---- ★ ----

She turned off a couple of lamps, then opened the front door and reached back and switched off the overhead lights. And suddenly she was slammed against the floor, was trying to scream, but a hand was pressed against her mouth. She kept struggling, writhing, kicking, but was being dragged to the back.

She could see, through a swimming blur, a man's shoes. He was straining back, didn't seem to know where to drag her, to the left, toward the front and now to the back again.

The cellar door!

He's opened it—she could tell by the squeaking.

The cellar!

He was dragging her to the top of the staircase. And suddenly she was falling, tumbling down the long wooden stairs.

She lay half-conscious on the cold concrete floor. She tried to get up in the blackness, kept trying, but failing.

She could hear him coming down, slowly.

---- ★ ----

"...a superb mystery that could happen to anyone."
— *The Snooper*

THE
GOOD
AND
THE
DEAD

SEYMOUR SHUBIN

WORLDWIDE.®

TORONTO • NEW YORK • LONDON
AMSTERDAM • PARIS • SYDNEY • HAMBURG
STOCKHOLM • ATHENS • TOKYO • MILAN
MADRID • WARSAW • BUDAPEST • AUCKLAND

THE GOOD AND THE DEAD

A Worldwide Mystery/October 2002

First published by Write Way Publishing, Inc.

ISBN 0-373-26436-4

Printed in U.S.A.

To Gloria

PROLOGUE

IT WAS WEIRD HOW, of all the thoughts of her whirling through his mind as he waited in the dark by her house, certain ones stood out. Of her skipping rope with the other girls, her skirt flapping above her knee-high socks, her little nose high—but she always held it high, even when she was just walking. Of that time when he was at the back of the line at the movies, the only kid there by himself, how she and the two other little bitches she was with would keep glancing back, pretending they were looking at something behind him, but their eyes always stopping a moment on him: how they would keep glancing back and then giggle at each other.

He'd belonged up there ahead of them and they knew it, knew he'd been right in front of them and had gone off just for a couple of seconds to buy some popcorn, but when he'd come back they were all crowded into each other, giggling, and he didn't have nerve enough to get back in, but went to the back of the line like a wimp.

And of all the times, the little blond-haired bitch, that little Goldilocks, she would walk by him without a look, would keep staring straight ahead or even turn away, though she was always playing up to all the other guys.

All these thoughts.

And so, after she had come out of the house and within frenzied seconds was dead, it came almost as a shock, as, staring down at her fully clothed body floating in the pool, he watched her hair fanning out on the water.

Long and black, and even with some strands of gray.

ONE

BEN NEWMAN STOOD just outside the lobby of his apartment building, waiting for his friend from Homicide to drive up from the street. The detective was about fifteen minutes late, which was unusual for him, but who knew, he could have been called away on a job. But a few minutes later, Ben saw McGlynn's green Chevy turn into the drive.

Ben walked around to the driver's side. He had timed his five-mile run almost perfectly and was still in his sweatshirt and shorts. McGlynn, a hefty man wearing a suit and a flowered, open shirt, rolled down his window.

"Kid," holding out his hand.

Ben took it. "Good to see you. I appreciate your coming over."

"Like I said, I was coming this way anyway." McGlynn lifted a manila envelope marked PHOTOS from the seat next to him and handed it to Ben. "Made copies, so you don't have to give 'em back. Got two angles of the two bodies, and there's some of the sleuths and one showing us bringing the bum out of his house."

"Great." He'd be sending them to New York. He had mailed off the article on these drug-related killings several days ago but McGlynn, who'd given him the story, hadn't been able to come up with pictures until now.

"And I'll see you tomorrow about the other thing." McGlynn often called murders "things." The case he was referring to involved a cab driver named Wilson who'd recently been sentenced to death for the rape and murder of a former fare's wife.

"I'll look forward to it."

McGlynn nodded and gave what, for him, was a smile. But it was only a very slight, tight movement of his lips.

THE MAN AT the security desk buzzed Ben through the glass doors into the inner lobby of his apartment building. He stood at the bank of elevators with an elderly woman; they smiled at each other but said nothing.

In the elevator she felt dwarfed standing next to him, though he wasn't quite six feet. Perhaps being thin but wide-shouldered, as if he trained at something all day, made him seem even taller. Whatever, he could still use a good meal, she thought. And a wife.

She'd heard he was single, which was a buzzword in the building. And he seemed to have it all—good looks, despite a nose that looked like it had been broken, nice hair the color of a beach, and young, about thirty or so. The only puzzlement was that he was a writer. Some kind of writer anyway, who worked with the police, with criminals.

Nobody she spoke to in the building seemed to really know, except a couple of people said he'd written at least one book. But he couldn't be doing too badly, could he, if he lived here? And in one of the penthouses yet?

THE PHONE was ringing as he walked into his apartment. He swept it up right before the answering machine took it, and sat down at his desk. "Hello."

"Ben? Carter."

Carter Svenson was editor-in-chief of the Gold Badge Magazine Group, in New York City, which consisted of four true detective magazines: *All-Clue Detective, Major Crimes Detective, Swift Justice Detective, and Pursuit Detective.* Carter was a man in his late seventies, who went back to the days, in the 'forties, when these magazines were among the kings of the newsstands. He was the only person Ben knew who still lit up one cigarette on the butt of another. "I'm calling mainly," he said, "about the Wilson case. You have any idea when I'll have it?"

"I just now spoke to a cop about it. I'm interviewing him tomorrow."

"That's fine, that's beautiful."

"He also brought over the pictures on the Thompson-Banders story. I'll Fed-Ex them overnight."

"All good news," Carter said.

They spoke of a few other crimes in and around Philadelphia that Ben was assigned to cover, and all the while he was staring out one of the picture windows at the Parthenon-like art museum only a short distance up the Benjamin Franklin Parkway. If he turned just a little to his left he would have a good view of the boat houses clustered along one side of the Schuylkill, some with eights and singles out on the river, with the downtown skyline a distant backdrop.

Hanging up, he went over to a table against the wall, whose lower rack was piled with magazines, most of them true detective, whose covers—melodramas all, some with scantily dressed beauties—were of people either in immediate danger or about to do harm while surrounded by such titles as BOSTON'S LONELY HEAD-HUNTER and KILL ME ONCE BUT NEVER TWICE, with, inside, all the psychic and avoid-hernia-surgery type ads.

He soon found what he was looking for, the name of an Ohio police officer he'd promised to fax to Carter.

His own stories were written under a variety of pen names; sometimes he had to use as many as three or four an issue. But during the past year he'd also gotten stories into *Vanity Fair* and *Harper's* magazines. And there was his book, which he just heard would be going into a third printing.

But he couldn't give up these mags yet.

BEN HAD NEVER READ one until a couple of weeks before he began writing for them.

He'd left Duke with a major in English, a goal of journalism but mostly with the idea that one day he would write books and articles on important things. He thought he might go on for a graduate degree in journalism, but decided to first take a year off and travel, and ended up in Caracas where he worked on an English language paper for another year. Then, wanting to come back to the states, he took a job as a reporter on a small paper in south Florida. He was soon assigned to police reporting, which he proved to be good at and which he liked. Then about four years later, after finishing a series of stories on a local triple murder by an elderly furniture finisher named Hallison, he got a call from someone named Carter Svenson, who said he'd read a couple of his stories on the Internet after they were brought to his attention by one of his editors. He wanted to know if Ben would like to do a story on the case for one of the Golden Badge Group magazines.

"To tell you the truth," Ben answered, "I've never read one."

"I don't have any doubts you can do it. If you're interested, let me send you a few copies and some guidelines. Only thing I ask is you get back to me fast with a yes or no."

The following day the package came to his apartment. It didn't take long for him to see that the magazines were interchangeable, and an analysis of the stories revealed a certain basic style. One of the most important things was to grab the reader in the first couple of paragraphs, and then to maintain as much suspense as possible until the killer was caught. As for the cases themselves, the guidelines said, they couldn't be "open and shut," such as someone recognizing the murderer as he or she left the scene. There had to be some degree of investigation, and the more suspects the better, though you didn't use the actual names of these people.

Ben sent the story off in a week, and the result was more assignments. Then one day, after hearing that Ben was originally from Philly, Carter asked him did he know anyone there who could cover the city for him, as well as other parts of Pennsylvania and much of New Jersey and Delaware. Ben said in essence hold on, and the next day, after some heavy thinking and deciding first one way and then another, he called back and took it.

He'd had no intention of staying at the paper "forever" anyway. And the thought of freelancing, of being on his own, and even the tensions of it, was appealing. He was young, this was an adventure, and, after all, the whole idea was to learn from it, from the experiences, the people—but never to forget that this was just another step along the way.

HE COULD HEAR the ringing of the phone while he was in the shower that night. But it stopped after the second ring.

Whoever it was didn't even wait for the answering machine to go on.

A few moments later it was ringing again, only to stop just as abruptly. Someone, he thought, was mighty impatient.

He came out to his combination living room-office, fixing the towel around his waist. Curious, he picked up the phone and tapped at the Star-69 buttons. The number he retrieved was his brother's. And it was busy now.

Ben sat at his desk, waiting for him to call again. Then he tried his number again, but it was still busy.

He turned on his computer and brought up the story he'd started yesterday and had finished a few hours ago.

ONE GOLD TOOTH FROM FREEDOM
By Tom Devers

Had he heard a moan?

The elderly handyman stared at the closed door of the bedroom, his heart suddenly racing. He had debated with himself about coming into the apartment, but the front door had been partly open and he had promised Miss McClatchy he would fix the leaking faucet in the bathroom. Maybe, he'd told himself, she had gone on an errand and had purposely left it open.

It was the morning of February 23,1928...

The handyman would enter the bedroom to find a dying, bludgeoned Miss McClatchy, who would mumble something about "missing mouth," which would prove to be that the killer had a missing gold tooth. Carter liked to have some of these old cases, which he called "historicals," on hand, should he need to fill space or, as he put it, "for balance."

Ben tried his brother again, then began printing out the story.

When he'd first come back to the city, four years ago, he'd moved into a small studio apartment, where the sofa turned into a bed and his computer stood on a bridge table. Here, he had a cleanly-functional mini-office by the long windows, next to the bookshelves that ran the length of the wall to the archway that opened to the bedroom and bathroom.

Sometimes it was still hard for him to believe he was buddies again with McGlynn and a lot of the other cops. Not only getting their stories again but once more being in their confidence, which had taken him so much time to win, and going out with them on arrests and raids and even on surveillances.

It had been maddening. To have a story already in print, the magazine out on the stands, and then to get this weird call from an ex-con for a meet, where you learn enough to suspect that a man you'd written about as a murderer in *All-Clue,* and who's now serving life, might not have done it after all. Then to look deeper into it, and then to go against all the cops you know and drink with and bullshit with, who, though you always pay them for their stories, let you know they'll never give you another one, even when it turns out to be true and the guy, Jerry Tomavich, walks. Even Carter, God, even *Carter* had said, "You know what the hell you're doing? You have any idea how much we can be sued for?"

But gradually, in the two years since then, the cops he'd worked with became friendly again, and there were some new ones as well, and Carter was happy that it had all turned into a PR plum. The book on his experience came through, as did the *Vanity Fair* and *Harper's* articles, all of which dealt in depth with the crimes he'd covered.

The phone was ringing. He swept it up. "Yes."

"Ben?" His brother's voice was thin, shaking.

"Harry, what's the matter?"

"Ben." Then, "My Pat. My beautiful Pat. She—she's gone. Dead."

And something, though Ben couldn't make out all the words, about his wife having an accident or being murdered, her body in their swimming pool.

And now as he sat with the phone down on his lap, Ben found himself staring numbly across the room. This was unreal, it couldn't be real. He wasn't aware for several long moments that his eyes had become fixed on those piles of magazines over there. And that it was as though they were spilling over, and flying open.

TWO

THEY STOOD, some fifty people, at the graveside in the late-April sun.

"A beautiful person in every way, an adoring and adored mother and wife, and a woman who I knew firsthand was always someone you could call on when there was a job to be done..."

Ben looked over at his brother, who'd let out a gasp at the Unitarian minister's words. Harry, his arm around his fifteen-year-old daughter, had begun crying again, softly, while she held on and cried with him. Sunlight slanting under the tent glinted off the length of the bronze casket.

How he hurt for them!

The minister was so right, Pat had been a beautiful person in every way. And to die so young, and so bizarrely!

"Dust to dust..."

The minister was handing his brother a little silvery spade. And after Harry and then Joannie sprinkled some dirt on the casket, and the funeral director announced that everyone was invited back to the house for lunch, people still seemed hesitant about leaving. Gradually they began drifting across the grass between the headstones to where the cars were parked on the gravel lane.

He looked to join Harry and Joannie in the walk to the limousine but others were with them. As he headed there he found himself seeking out a young woman he'd noticed earlier. He had spotted her as they'd flocked here from the cars—in fact, she had been looking at him, then averted her eyes. There had been something familiar about that face but he had no idea where he had seen her before.

Now he saw that she was standing near the cars, looking at him as he approached. She walked part way to him.

"Hi. Do you remember me? Ellen Packler?"

For a moment the name, the thin bony face, meant nothing. Then somehow the face became a very young face, was filling out a little, and the reddish hair became blond. And what he felt all at once wasn't so much a wave of recognition but a jolt of recognition and delight.

"Ellen! Of course. Of course." He reached out for her hand. She'd gone through school with him, elementary and senior high. But he wondered what he'd recognized about her. Maybe the eyes; that, and the mouth. She couldn't be more than thirty, thirty-one, but she looked so much older.

"I want to say," she said, "it's good to see you. But it's an awful place and time to say that."

"It is good seeing you," he said. He released her hand.

"I'm so sorry about Pat," she said.

He nodded. What the hell could you say?

"Do they say…I—I don't mean to pry, but does anyone know what happened?"

"We really don't know." Which was true. Harry had come home that night to an empty house, their daughter had been sleeping at a friend's. A few lights were on, including one on the back patio. When he walked out there, he saw her floating face up in the swimming pool. There was a deep bruise on her forehead, which could have been from a fall on the concrete deck. It was possible she'd stumbled and knocked herself out and rolled into the pool. She hadn't been sexually attacked, and nothing was missing from her person or from the house. From some newspapers scattered about near the trash cans, police theorized that she may have walked outside to do some picking up.

"It's so horrible, so unbelievable," Ellen said. "You know, this is the part that almost drives me crazy—I was with her that night. In fact, I drove her home."

"Oh my."

"I can't get it out of my head. I want you to know she talked about you. In fact she used to talk about you quite a bit. She was so proud when you, you know, what you did, getting that poor man out of prison." She paused. "I've got your book, by the way."

"So it's you. My publisher calls me every time one sells."

She smiled fleetingly. "What she said— I don't know whether you've heard, but Barwyn's going to be celebrating its bicentennial." Barwyn was the section of the city where he'd lived until he had gone off to college. "We've been helping out, writing a history. She said that night she was going to ask your advice…just that night," she repeated.

"I heard something about the bicentennial, but Pat never mentioned anything." He shook his head. "It's all so damn sad, so unbelievable. Are you coming back to the house? I wish you would; there's so much to catch up on.''

But she shook her head. "No, I can't. I wish I could but I can't. Well…'' She held out her hand again. ''I only wish that after all these years we could have seen each other at a happy time.''

Almost everyone came back to Harry's two-story, stone Colonial house in the Chestnut Hill section of the city, and to a dining room table covered to the edges with food—a sliced baked ham and roast beef, mounds of potato salad and macaroni salad, snowflake rolls, relishes, cakes—all of it supplied by neighbors. A huge coffee urn stood on the sideboard, along with bottles of soda and liquor. People were eating from paper plates on their laps or while standing. There was steady conversation and here and there even a trace of a smile.

Ben wanted to be with Harry but he was sitting over in a corner, three people around him, talking to him as he sat silent and gray-faced. He was eight years older than Ben; a cardiologist. And poor, dazed-looking Joannie, almost the image of Pat with her long black hair and perfectly straight nose, was on the sofa between Pat's mother and father, holding their hands.

This is such a bitch, he kept thinking. It was so goddamn sad and such a goddamn horror.

Those two, Harry and Pat, had had something that was almost too special. It had started when they were no more than thirteen and it had driven both families crazy—Harry'd go to dances at her church, and sometimes on High Holidays she'd even be waiting on the sidewalk for him to come out of synagogue. Finally they eloped, right after Harry entered med school.

It had worked out beautifully. After all these years they'd still seemed like one in so many ways, and of course they'd long ago reconciled with their families.

Two of the people around Harry walked off, but three others took their place.

Ben walked over to the urn and poured himself a cup of coffee. He wasn't at all hungry, felt hollowed out. He knew only a few people here: most were friends of Pat's and Harry's, and Pat's relatives, some of whom he'd never met. Only a couple of his relatives were still here, his only aunt and uncle. He had talked to them earlier.

They drifted back over to him. They looked lost. Uncle Irv, his father's younger brother, had something of his father's face, but his eyes were thick-lidded and always sad. His aunt, a heavy little woman, always had a vague smile, even now.

"So, Ben," his uncle said heavily. And though he'd said this before: "So, your book, I hear it's doing real well."

"Not bad."

"That's good, that's good." Then, nodding toward Harry, "I feel so bad, so sorry. She was such a nice lady."

"She was gold," his aunt offered. "I loved her. And I know your mother and father did, may they rest in peace. They used to say it so many times."

"And no one knows what happened," his uncle said hesitantly. Then when Ben didn't say anything, "Well, I guess we're going to have to go."

"You two take care of yourselves." Ben shook his uncle's hand. Though his father had been a much better-looking man, there was enough of a resemblance that it was as though he were having a final look at his father. He embraced his aunt lightly and kissed her on the cheek. She touched the back of his head and said, ''You're so handsome, I can't believe some girl hasn't...''

''Don't worry about him,'' his uncle said.

''I'm not worried about him, I'm worried about the girls,'' and she smiled and pressed her hand hard against his cheek. When they left, first stopping to say goodbye to Harry, he saw his brother looking at him. Then Harry stood up and came over. ''Ben, I'd like to talk to you.''

Ben was surprised when he saw he was supposed to follow Ben upstairs. He felt a sense of anxiety and it started to flare a little more as Harry led him into his bedroom and closed the door. They didn't look at all like brothers: Harry was much shorter than Ben, chunky, with black hair balding in back. It added to the feeling Ben always had that Harry was more like a second father to him.

Harry leaned back against the bureau. His face, Ben saw with even greater uneasiness, had become fiery; he didn't seem to know what to do with his hands, kept rubbing at his wrists. Then his eyes filled up and he looked at the floor.

''Ben, they think— I'm sure the police think I killed her.''

Ben felt a sudden hot sagging in his chest. ''What the hell you talking about?''

''They think it, they suspect it. I know.''

''What do you mean you know?''

''The cops have just about said it. The autopsy showed she didn't have a heart attack; they couldn't find any reason she collapsed.''

''She could have just tripped, hit her head—''

"There was nothing she could have tripped on. They say it's strange she didn't have any bruises on her hands, her arms—that you'd think she would have thrown up her arms to protect herself if she was falling. They're sure someone surprised her, maybe knocked her out, then held her under the water."

Ben said, after a long moment, "All right, so their first thought is you. You know as well as I do the spouse is the first one they always think of. It's perfectly normal, routine."

But it was as though Harry didn't hear. "One of the things they asked me, they asked if we always uncovered the pool this early. And I told them the truth, that I took it off because I wanted to have something done to the pool. But I never got around to calling anyone."

"So you never got around to it. So?"

Harry looked at him. Then he lowered his eyes again, was staring at the floor as he said, "Ben, I've been seeing someone."

Oh, Christ! Harry? Harry fucking around? He managed to say quietly, "You want to tell me?"

Harry shrugged without looking up: "It's, uh, it's someone I've been seeing for a while."

Christ, Ben couldn't even think of questions; he was all confused. "Was it serious?"

"Not on my part."

"Did Pat know?"

"That night—that night's the first time I think she suspected something. Or maybe even knew. She was...different. Snapped at me over—you know, nothing, really nothing. I made up a story, but then she asked me a couple minutes later where I was going, what time I was coming back. She never did that before. Never like that, anyway."

"Where were you going?"

Harry kept staring at the floor; it was answer enough. Then he lowered his face to his hands. "Ben— The detectives asked me where I was that night. And like an ass, like a jackass, I made up some stupid, stupid lie."

THREE

HARRY LOOKED UP slowly; his chin was quivering, his eyes brimming with tears. "God forgive me, Ben. I loved her. God only knows how I loved her. I don't know why I didn't know how good I had it."

Ben came over to him. He felt like shaking the hell out of him but instead put his hands gently on his forearms. "I know you loved her. You don't have to tell me."

"Then why"—Harry was shaking his head slowly-"why did I, why— And now I'm so scared, Ben. I don't give a shit about myself. Honest to God, I swear. But I don't want Joannie to ever know."

"Try to calm down." Ben put his arms around Harry, aware that he couldn't remember the last time either of them had done this. "Come on, try to calm down. Come on, buddy."

Ben could feel Harry's breathing gradually start to ease. But his own heart was still going hard. It wasn't, he knew, only because of what Harry told him. It was that his brother had opened up to him at *all*. This just wasn't Harry, not with him. They rarely if ever confided in each other about anything. It went back to when Ben was a kid, when he felt no more free to talk to Harry about personal things, sex for sure, than to his father.

And even now, even though they lived in the same city, they hardly saw each other.

"I'll be all right," Harry said. He nodded and let his arms drop from Ben.

"Let's sit down."

Harry sank onto a chair, his head down. Ben sat on the edge of the bed, looking at him.

"I should have told the police the truth. I know it, you don't have to tell me. But I didn't want Joannie to know. And—and I was afraid it would be all over the papers and what the police would do with it. I panicked."

"What did you tell them?"

"That I'd been at the hospital late and then went back to my office and stayed until about eleven, all of which is true except I said I went there to work on a paper."

"You really doing a paper?"

He nodded. "I can show them something if I have to."

"You think anyone saw you with her?"

"No. I was very careful about that."

As Ben knew, it wasn't as if his office was in a busy building; he and another physician shared a converted brownstone.

"Do you think she's told anyone she's been seeing you?"

"I don't know why she would. No, I'm positive not. She's married."

"I'm not asking her name, I don't want to know her name, but did she know Pat? Was she one of your friends?"

Harry shook his head. "I met her at the bank; she's one of the tellers. She really was nothing to me. Nothing." Tears were sliding down his face again. Elbows on his knees, he held his hands to his forehead.

After a few moments Ben said, "Harry?" Harry looked up slowly. "I'm not telling you what to do, I'm just asking. What if you go see the cops? What if you tell them?"

Harry grimaced, his eyes wide. "You kidding? You crazy? Christ, you crazy?"

And there it was, the old Harry—say one word he didn't like and he'd chew your head off.

"I'm just asking," patiently, "I'm just saying."

"I *can't.* Don't you understand? I'm afraid I'll only make it worse. And maybe they won't even find out." He lowered his head again. "I just can't."

Ben looked at him, at his bald spot and the bulk of his cheeks; he'd gotten heavier this past year. He felt a surge of anger at that helpless-looking figure, which he'd been trying to suppress, wanted to say *Look, they're only gonna find out! Look, you son of a bitch, they're only—*

But Harry was looking up in a pitiful way that would have stopped him anyway. "Ben," he said pleadingly, "you work with the police. Do you know the two detectives who were here? Lafferty? The other was Dauber?"

THE FIRST THING he did when he got back to his apartment was throw his suit jacket on the sofa and then wash his face, hard, more to try to get the tension out of his head than anything else. But nothing was going to ease it.

He couldn't stop thinking of Harry asking if he knew the detectives who'd questioned him. He didn't, though he did know that a Lafferty was in Homicide, and he assumed from where Harry lived that this Dauber was from the Northwest Detective Division. It was weird how Harry, always the big brother, was suddenly seeing him with the kind of power where he could go to the cops and assure them of his innocence.

He got a bottle of Evian from the refrigerator and stood with it by the window. The sky was turning pink-gray, and early lights were on throughout the city. He took a swallow of water and set the bottle down. He'd gone for a run early that morning, up the West River Drive, with the sun on the Schuylkill, then through the woods and hills of Fairmount Park, where he'd joined up with a few high school cross-country kids; and he'd run along with them for a while, until he broke off and ran alone. Now he felt disturbed and restless enough to want to run again.

He didn't let himself think that Harry might be lying. Or at least not think of it for more than a few seconds. It was impossible that Harry would have ever hurt her, it was crazy.

And yet he wondered should he try something he'd been thinking about, or if he would only be stirring up more trouble.

Occasionally during the day his mind had drifted back to Ellen Packler at the cemetery, thinking of the stark physical change in her and wondering how things had gone with her since high school. But it was on the ride back here to his apartment that he'd thought of something else.

If Harry was right, Pat hadn't seemed to suspect anything that night—the night she went out with Ellen. So there was a good chance that if she hadn't mentioned anything to Ellen, she hadn't to anyone else. That it had died with her.

He couldn't just *ask* Ellen, of course. But he had this thing in his head that if he could see her, that somehow after they were finished talking about the old days and the new, she might tell him, or at least hint at, if Pat had mentioned anything. Or even if she'd *looked* troubled.

He wasn't sure what he was going to do, even as he reached for the phone book. Furthermore, he was pretty sure he'd seen a wedding ring, so probably the only way he could come up with a listing was if it happened to be under her maiden name.

There was nothing in Philly. And nothing, Information told him, in the few suburbs he tried. He sat back, disappointed, but for a moment it had little to do with Harry; mostly, that he would have liked to talk with her.

Funny, they'd probably started in kindergarten together, but though he had vague images of her through the years, the only one that really stood out was in high school. She'd been a beauty, slender, with straight blond hair and a slightly upturned nose. And a brain—one of those who they announce at graduation had gotten all A's forever; and she'd been class vice president, if he remembered correctly, and had been either the valedictorian or salutatorian.

Someone he'd looked on as unreachable, at least to him, until the class trip up the Hudson River to West Point. It had been later that night, when he left the dancing to get a breather at the rail. After awhile she showed up, close by, standing there looking at the water in the other direction. Then she asked him something, like what did he like most about the trip, and soon they were talking about which college they were going to, and he was telling her what he liked about

Duke, and she was going to Smith. Then they took a little walk together, then stopped, and she turned and looked at him, and he put his arms around her. Her lips opened almost immediately as they kissed. It certainly wasn't his first soul kiss but, her body pressing against him, there'd been no tongue like it, to each side of his mouth, the roof, searching deeper, then drawing his in. It was instant, unbelievable love, there on the river, with even the moon on the dark ripples.

But as it turned out she was going steady with Jim Raymond, the co-captain of the soccer team. That was the end of that.

He wondered did she end up with Jim Raymond.

Harry surely knew where she lived, but he didn't want to ask him unless there was no alternative. He tried New Jersey Information this time, but nothing there. He tried the phone book again on the chance he'd overlooked it. No. But then, scanning further down the P columns, his eyes swiftly focused on a name he had either skipped or misread: Packler-Woods.

Packler-Woods, E., Dr.

It seemed so right that she should be a doctor—he had no doubt it was her. He felt happy for her; it would have been a pity not to do something with those brains.

He glanced at his watch—it was after seven—then dialed quickly. And she answered.

"Ellen," he said. "Ben Newman."

There was a pause, then a delighted, "Oh, Ben, how good to hear from you."

"I was sorry you couldn't come back to the house. I wish we'd had a chance to talk. So I thought I'd call."

"I'm glad you did." She paused, then said it again, "I'm glad you did. How nice."

"Am I catching you at a wrong time? You with a patient?"

"No, not at all. The right time. I'm between patients. It's really nice to hear from you."

"I was just wondering about something. You mentioned a history you and Pat were writing."

"Yes, we collected a lot of material and put together a very rough draft, which is what Pat wanted to talk to you about."

He said, "Well, I want you to know if there's any way I can still help, I'll be happy to."

"Would you? Oh my. I'd love for you to look at it. I've got most of it Xeroxed. I could mail it to you."

"If you'd like, and have some time this evening or tomorrow, I'll be glad to go over it with you. You wouldn't need to mail it."

"Really?" she said. "This evening?"

DURING THE FOUR YEARS he'd been back in the city he had never had any reason to be in Barwyn; at most, he'd driven along its fringes. Now, driving through the heart of it, he felt surge after surge of recognition. It felt so much longer than fifteen years since he'd lived here, and a part of him had been anticipating some great changes. But no. The houses stood there as if he were still a kid barely noticing them, most of them old rowhouses or twins, with open, pillared porches facing a small patch of lawn. Most of the streets were bordered sparsely with trees.

He'd half-expected graffiti but he hadn't seen any so far.

Yet he really wasn't surprised, especially after Ellen

had told him she still lived here. It had always been that kind of community, where a lot of each generation stayed on. He could remember kids in grammar school telling him their parents or even grandparents had gone to the same school, maybe even had some of the same teachers. It used to amaze him. He'd had trouble even visualizing his parents' early lives. Older than most of his friends' parents, they had been taken out of Germany as children right before the war, and had met and married here.

He was a little early; Ellen wasn't expecting him until a quarter to eight. He drove through the deepening night to his old street. He slowed up at his house, a twin with an enclosed, many-windowed porch and a small, hedge-bordered lawn. He stopped briefly and stared down the alley along the house that led to the driveway where the kids used to play ball. This time of year his mother might be out on the ladder, washing the first-floor windows, and it would start to be light out when his father came home from his mattress store downtown.

He never went in that house again after he left for college; his parents had moved into an apartment. They died a few years later, within months of each other.

He drove on, went past the large cathedral-like Lutheran church that poor Pat had gone to, and then past the small, beige-stone synagogue a few blocks away. He wouldn't have been surprised if it wasn't there anymore. When he was a kid, and probably still now, a large percentage of the people in Barwyn were of German descent. And there used to be, at most, only two or three Jews in his class in grade school. High school, though, there had been a lot more—kids came there from other sections of the city.

Heading toward Ellen's he went past the high school, Barwyn High: five floors of dun-colored brick and half-shaded windows, with a vast expanse of yard in back and its athletic field across the street. It had been built in the early 'thirties, which made it almost brand new compared to Barwyn Elementary, which went back to the mid-eighteen hundreds. Again he was driving slowly, looking it over. It was surprising how little of its interior he could remember—the gym, he could picture the gym and the humid, boisterous locker rooms and the hushed auditorium. But now some of the classrooms were starting to come back, and the lunchroom, and now some of the faces of the teachers he'd thought he would never forget—like Miss Cromley, who'd made Latin a misery, and Mrs. Henry, who'd made English a joy, and Cobble, the gym teacher who'd make you "assume the angle" if you did something wrong, which meant bending over and holding your ankles while he kicked you once or twice on the ass with the side of his sneakered foot.

He should get going, it was almost quarter of, but he felt pulled to see Barwyn Elementary. It was only a few blocks away. He circled it slowly, a two-story, dark-stone building encircled by its yard, almost sullen-looking even with kids' drawings on the windows. It had been almost twenty years since he'd been in there. He remembered even less of what it looked like inside than the high school, mostly that the boys' room was in the whitewashed basement, and so was the lunchroom, and the classroom blackboards opened up to make auditoriums, and that you needed a long pole to open and close the windows. But it was mostly

feelings he remembered, like how it felt standing outside in lines before entering in the morning, and putting covers on books, and finally in the seventh
grade—the school went through the eighth—going to
different teachers instead of having just one. And
everyone in the eighth grade suddenly being such big
shots.

He got so caught up that for a few moments he
forgot how to get to Ellen's, and then was a little surprised to see the first graffiti. But this stopped soon,
and then in the light of the street lamps things became
recognizable again: he saw the Catholic church, then
the luncheonette (it was still a luncheonette though the
sign didn't say Elmers anymore), then the firehouse.
And down this corner he was passing was the library,
and just ahead the Barwyn Theater, and he knew to
turn on this street here.

He found Ellen's address to be a corner storefront.
The sign came as a surprise, a letdown: Dr. Ellen
Packler-Woods, Podiatrist. He'd assumed she was an
MD, couldn't quite picture the Ellen Packler he knew
back then working on feet.

Turning off the lights and motor, he sat looking over
at the door. He'd started feeling anxious about this
long before he left the house, but nothing like now,
that this was an awful mistake, that he was going to
hear something Pat had told her that he didn't want to
hear; that somehow this visit might even stir things up
disastrously. He was almost unaware for a moment
that his hand was going to the car door handle.

He tried her door, then pressed the buzzer. Her
voice asked over the intercom who it was, and then
brightened a little and said wait in the waiting room,
she'd be finished soon. The waiting room was empty.

He looked at a couple of abstract prints over the brown leather sofa, then sat down on one of the contoured chairs.

He was wearing an old but favorite camelhair sports jacket over jeans, and an open shirt. He had made himself wear socks.

He could feel himself calming down, but still felt a sense of unreality—not only that he was back in Barwyn, but where, with whom.

She came out in a few minutes with a patient, smiled at Ben and then spoke with the patient at the door. She came over to Ben and held out her hand.

"I'm glad you were able to come over," she said.

"I was looking forward to it."

"Let me get rid of this," she said, taking off her lab coat.

She went into the back briefly. Then they angled two chairs so they could sit close, facing each other. There was a trace of premature gray at the roots of her hair and her thin throat showed loosening skin above her white blouse. Still, despite the bony face, it had become easier to see the school girl's face.

"I'm still in shock over Pat," she said. "And what makes it even more horrible is that it's the second funeral of a friend of mine I've been to in the past three weeks. In fact, of course, you knew him. God, how could it slip my mind? George Havers? You remember George, don't you?"

"Of course." From school too, all the way through elementary and high. A real nice kid, a real good guy.

"That was awful too. He committed suicide."

"Oh, Jesus. No."

"Absolutely horrible. I hadn't seen him since high school but then a few years ago he married a friend of mine. He seemed to have it so good. He was a druggist, had his own store, a nice home, two beautiful babies. Sharon adored him. And then he hangs himself. She still can't accept it—'George wouldn't do it, there was no reason.' I agree, but he did it. I spoke to her today—she's going to drive herself mad.''

''That's damn sad.''

George Havers. He repeated the name in his mind with a real sense of sadness. A terrific kid, bright, nice, really *nice,* and a tremendous athlete. Ben had always been a good athlete himself, particularly in wrestling and swimming—that's how he broke his nose, on the water polo team in college—but George had been the star of just about every team he was on, ever since they were little guys. And made all-city guard his last two years in high school. Could still see him, the last real memory he had of him, picking up a fumble and running over eighty-two yards to the two.

''What a damn shame.'' It seemed so inadequate.

''So that's been my past few weeks,'' Ellen said. ''First George, then Pat.''

They sat quietly, somberly, thinking. Then Ben said, ''Had you known Pat long?''

Ellen explained that she used to see her around when Pat lived in Barwyn, but only got to know her well in the past six months or so. Pat's family's roots here went way back to the early eighteen hundreds; her father used to be president of the Chamber of Commerce. So when the Chamber began planning the bicentennial, Pat was one of those they'd called on to serve on a committee—and Pat had asked her to help with the history of Barwyn.

And then Ellen said it so easily, so naturally, that for an instant Ben forgot he had been worried: ''They were such a wonderful couple, she and Harry. What a terrible tragedy.''

He drew in a quiet breath of relief.

"THIS," ELLEN SAID, carrying a thick folder from her office, "is as far as we got."

She placed it on a low table in front of the sofa and they began going through it. Slowly he turned the pages of the ringed book that held the typed first draft, then looked at some of the materials they'd drawn from or hadn't used as yet. "This, for instance," she pointed out, "is a diagram of the area in the late seventeen-hundreds; see, one family owned all these miles and miles of land." This was a cotton mill, long gone. Here, a daguerreotype of the first farm houses, then the first shops. Two Civil War soldiers. Four more. An iron factory. Families staring rigidly at the camera. A history of the first English settlers, a sketch of the first Lutheran church. An article on the early Germans, another on the early English. An oral history of Alfred Barwyn, whom the town was named after. Newspaper clippings of Barwynites in the major wars. And material on the more recent influxes into the area: Asians, African-Americans, Hispanics.

"It's too much to read now," she said, "so if you'd like, take it along."

She wanted to know something of what he'd done after leaving college, and after he told her she said, "And you're not married. I know that. Pat told me.

"My God, I can't believe it. She forgot that whole ceremony."

She smiled, the first he'd seen her really smile, and when he said, "Now tell me about you," she indicated with her hands that there wasn't much to say. She'd gotten a scholarship to Smith, a real dream come true, and had hoped to go on to med school. But then the blow—her folks couldn't afford it. Finally, after she got married, and before they had the baby, she went to podiatry college.

"I like it, I really do," she said. She was smiling again, but it was a little sad, he thought.

"Do you see any of the old gang?"

"Let's see." She named a couple he didn't remember, then one that he certainly did—Dan Haupt, his best friend in grammar school. God, they'd been so close—the closest. Practically lived in each other's houses, did everything together.

He said, "Do you know where he lives?"

"Here in Barwyn. He took over his father's store."

How well he remembered that store—Haupt's Hardware and Paints. But he was a little surprised that Danny was running it. He used to talk so determinedly about being an architect.

Ellen looked at her watch. "Would you like to stop at the house?"

"Thanks, but I think I'll get going."

They stood up together and she went in back for a coat. By now some way-early memories had come back. He remembered her as Priscilla—how could he have forgotten?—and he an Indian. He remembered her on one of the parents' visiting days—he knew which because it was one of two where his mother came, his father could never make it—and how Ellen kept shooting up her arm in answer to every question. He even remembered her in kindergarten, sitting next to him as they sat around Miss Blauman as she played the piano, and Miss Blauman never aware that the white V of her panties was showing. And Ellen with a pink dress—he remembered

her with that dress that showed her knees, chest totally
flat, and then one day watching her running and seeing
a little bounce of breasts. But after that all he could
remember of her was in high school: in the one class
they shared, but mostly the times he'd see her in the
cafeteria or walking in the hall, in a sweater usually, her
books hugged to her breast.

He wondered if, as they'd been talking, she had
thought of that time on the Hudson.

"I'll be right there," she called.

He wasn't sure why, but he felt a little sorry for her.
It was the business about med school of course, but
not only that; maybe it had to do mostly with Barwyn,
the thought of staying on here, among the same
houses, the same faces.

She came out carrying a light coat and a briefcase.
She'd told him earlier that she lived right up the block;
her husband was the service manager at an auto
agency, and they had a seven-year-old daughter.

He said, "I'll walk with you."

"Oh, fine."

She opened the door, then reached in and turned off
the last lights. He looked on as she made sure the door
was locked. She turned and smiled. As they walked
down the steps to the sidewalk, a car's headlights went
on a short distance down the street; its brights. But he
barely noticed until the car came closer, then slowed
up for a few moments, its beams on them, before
speeding on.

FOUR

BEN CALLED HARRY the next morning and learned from his mother-in-law, who was staying on to look after Joannie, that he'd gone to see a few patients in the hospital. He wouldn't be putting in a full day, though; he'd said he'd be back in a couple of hours.

Putting down the phone, Ben felt a kind of relief, as though things had taken a long stride back to normal. But he knew it was deceiving. Until his brother was cleared, it would feel like the cops were holding onto his ankles.

For what felt like the thousandth time, he asked himself who could have murdered Pat. Who? And why? It wasn't robbery, it wasn't sex. Perhaps she'd accidentally come upon an intruder, but why kill her?

He couldn't blame the cops for thinking it might be her husband. But—except for a few terrible seconds when he himself had to fight it—he would bet his life against it.

He looked out the window at the flow of cars along the Expressway bordering the Schuylkill. He stared over at the art museum, wishing he had peace of mind enough to go there. Then, almost with a force of will, he rolled his chair in front of the computer.

Detective McGlynn had come over a few days ago, as he'd promised, and given him the facts and some photos of the case of the cab driver, Wilson, who killed the wife of one of his fares. But he hadn't touched it yet; hadn't been able to give it the concentration to even start it.

He arranged his notes and scanned them, pausing to read some two or three times. The cab driver, a married man of forty-one, had first seen the victim's wife when he had helped carry the man's luggage into the house. Three days later he had come back and raped and murdered her. He was now under sentence of death.

Opening the computer screen, Ben tried to think of a good first paragraph. He generally never started with a title, but afterward would come up with a list of possibles on a separate page, knowing that Carter just about never used anyone else's. The old guy, who had edited not just these detective things but aviation magazines and a couple of dozen other types over the years, looked on his own terrible titles as a kind of art work.

Ben kept staring from the screen to his notes.

Whatever he had written about in the past, the murdered dead, killers, death-scenes, mourning families, he'd written at a distance. But he was never aware of that distance more than now. Nor closer to some of the titles.

He knew he had to fight through this.

But when he thought of a body it was Pat's body. And when he thought of a murderer, Harry's face kept breaking in.

HE WAS THREE PAGES into the story when he had to lean back away from it. He couldn't shake Harry from his head. He was so goddamn mad at him and yet so scared.

Scared for him more than anything.

What were the police planning on doing with him?

He could ask McGlynn did he know anything, hear anything. And Ben did know someone at the 14th, Herm Nelson.

It was so tempting to reach for the phone, to say something like, "Look, I don't know if you know but my brother is… Is there anything you can tell…?"

And yet it wasn't tempting at all.

It was crazy and would accomplish nothing.

Except put him with his brother in that world the cops loathed.

JOANNIE CALLED about an hour and a half later, urgency in her voice. "Uncle Ben, did you hear from Daddy?"

"No." He felt a sudden rush of tension. "Has something happened?"

"No, it's just he's not home yet."

He glanced quickly at his watch. "It's only after ten, honey, it's early."

"I—I know. But he left real early. Like seven. He said he'd be back by nine. I don't know, he looked terrible."

"Sweetheart, you really aren't giving him much time."

"I guess. I—I'm sorry. But I just got worried."

"Don't be sorry. But try not to worry, that's all I'm saying. He's fine, he's at the hospital. You know how it is there."

"I know."

"Now try to remember that. Call me when he gets in."

When he didn't hear after a couple of hours, he called there. "No," Harry's mother-in-law told him, "still no word. All we've heard is that he left the hospital about eight-thirty."

"Well, I'm sure it's nothing," but he was worried himself now. Where the hell was he?

Lowering the phone, he wondered should he go to Harry's house? He wanted to but was afraid his showing up would completely panic them. He'd give it another hour—a half hour.

Almost at that moment there was a buzz and then Harry's voice came over the intercom from outside.

"Ben. Me. Can I come up?"

"What do you mean can you come up?" Christ! "Of course come up."

Ben, blood pulsing into his face, waited by the open door. The first thing he noticed as Harry walked toward him from the elevators was that his face was almost plaster white. His suit jacket hung open; its lapel was partly crumpled in.

"Harry, what's the matter?"

But his brother said nothing as he walked in. He just seemed to want to get inside. Looking at Ben he sank slowly in a chair. "They…they found out about her. Someone, I don't know who, someone told them about-about us. And they know I lied, that I was with her."

Above the rocketing of his heart: "How'd you find out?"

"They had me down there, at the station. What do you think I'm saying?"

How the hell would I know, Ben thought, glaring at him, but this was Harry. This was *Harry!*

"It was awful. They questioned me for more than two hours. They asked me first did I want a lawyer and I said no. I felt…I felt if you ask for a lawyer it means you're saying you're guilty. But they treated me like *I was* guilty. They didn't come right out and accuse me of anything; but they asked me the same things over and over. It's what they think. You'd have to be a moron not to know it."

Ben stared at Harry as he sat with his forehead resting on his hand. "Look, Harry, listen to me." He kneeled next to him. "Just listen. They know about her—good, it's out now. The worst of it is over. It's over."

Harry's hand came down slowly. Then he shook his head. "There's something else I was just too flustered, too scared, to tell them. A lot of my investments have gone really sour this past year. So what I did, to protect Pat should anything happen to me, was take out additional life insurance. And it was Pat's idea that I also insure her; she'd never had life insurance before."

Ben was almost afraid to ask. "How much was it for?"

"Over a quarter million. But I don't want a penny of it, not a penny—"

Ben had to sit down to control himself. He wanted to grab Harry, shake him, even punch him. *Didn't you tell them, you dumb fucking bastard? How could you think for a second they wouldn't dig into your whole history?*

ELLEN PACKLER-WOODS, her last patient gone, went to her desk to straighten it out, then looked again at some X-rays she'd just taken. Definitely no tumor; a change to thick-soled shoes and pads should alleviate the poor woman's discomfort. She slipped them back in the folder and filed them away, then opened some junk mail that had been there since morning. She leaned back after awhile, aware she was holding off going home.

Her husband would have a late dinner waiting—he almost always did the cooking when she came home late. A big-bellied man, he enjoyed cooking—the pity was, she was a small eater.

Her daughter would have already eaten and was surely in her room—Ellen hoped doing homework, but probably on the computer or phone.

She thought of Ben, as she'd occasionally done during the day. There had always been something nice about him, quiet and nice, and he certainly hadn't lost it over the years. What she remembered of him from grade school was a thin kid, real blond then, one of the best students, who was so quiet she was sometimes surprised when she'd see him out in the yard laughing and wrestling and roughing it up with the fellows. And "nice-looking"—when she'd thought about him at all it was as nice-looking, but not "real cute," the highest compliment; and it didn't become more than that until one day when they were juniors in high school, a few of the girls, looking over at him in the cafeteria, said isn't he good-looking?

She thought of the trip up the Hudson and how she'd left the dancing to try to "accidentally" find him. And those clear blue eyes as they talked, and the long, passionate kiss.

It was strange how, sitting here talking with him, she hadn't felt the slightest bit uncomfortable about it.

She was sure it had something to do with him, his whole manner.

But the thing she still felt terribly **une**asy about was having lied about med school; had the feeling he wouldn't have thought any less of her for not getting in because of her grades. It had all started at Smith when this brain from Barwyn, who'd never been away from home, came up against all those other brains. Shock turned into fear, and fear into panic; and then she became anorectic, somehow thinking that being as bony as a skull was beautiful; and soon the scholarship went away, she had to come home, and then a couple of years later was finally well enough to start up again at Temple, in the city.

She stood up from her desk and went to the closet for her coat. She held it for a few moments.

What would it have been like if she'd gone out with him after the trip? Probably nothing, just a date, just some dates, and the two of them would have moved on the way they did. But it could have been—who knows?—like any road you take instead of another.

No matter. There'd never been a question of her going out with him. It was dreadful but true.

"*Jewish?*" She could just see her mother and father, particularly her mother, saying it.

What's worse, she herself had felt it.

She swung on her coat.

How she admired him. It wasn't just for the book, though it was that. And it wasn't just for saving someone from prison, going against the so-called establishment, though it was very much that, too. Very simply, from where she was locked into Barwyn, it was for going out in the world and doing something.

She pulled a kerchief from her pocket because it

had gotten a little windy, then decided against it and stuffed it back. She went over to her desk again to see about bringing home some journals, but changed her mind. She'd wash her hair, watch some TV.

She put out the lights in the examination room. In the waiting room, she turned off a couple of lamps, then opened the front door and reached back and switched off the overhead lights. And suddenly she was slammed against the floor, was trying to scream, but a hand was pressed against her mouth. She kept struggling, writhing, kicking, but was being dragged to the back.

She could see, through a swimming blur, a man's shoes. He was straining back, didn't seem to know where to drag her, to the left, toward the front and now to the back again.

The cellar door!

He'd opened it—she could tell by the squeaking.

The cellar!

He was dragging her to the top of the staircase. And suddenly she was falling, tumbling down the long wooden stairs.

She lay half-conscious on the cold concrete floor. She tried to get up in the blackness, kept trying, but falling back.

She could hear him coming down, slowly. And now he was lifting her up.

She was like a baby in his arms.

And then she felt herself dropping in air, felt the first cut of the steps, was rolling. And now nothing at all.

FIVE

JUST FOUR STREETS AWAY, on a block of two-story, narrowly separated Victorian-style homes, lived one of the legends of the community of Barwyn. Her name was Catherine Cassaway. A "single lady," she had lived in the same house for sixty of her sixty-four years. She had been teaching seventh-grade English at Barwyn Elementary School, her first and only job, since she was twenty-two. Although she could have retired long ago she was still not even contemplating it.

She was a medium-weight woman of about five-six who somehow gave the illusion of being taller, with pulled-back, ash-gray hair that, once shiny black, was the most prominent change most students from long ago noticed about her. Her face, amazingly almost wrinkle-free, had a touch of pink to it though she had never used makeup. Her nose was straight above thin, dry lips, her chin jutting, giving her the patrician look of an ancient Roman bust.

She gave off such an aura of sternness, and stories about her in the classroom were such that even neighbors would often find themselves a touch relieved when she smiled.

On this morning she had neither read a paper yet nor heard the news, so was unaware of the death last

night of Ellen Packler-Woods. An hour away from
leaving for school, she was looking out at her back
garden as she sipped her tea. The hyacinth and crocus
were out, and soon the azaleas, clustered in thick
bushes along the front of her house, should begin to
show buds. The thought made her a little sad. Her
mother, dead three years now at the age of eighty-six,
used to take particular delight in the azaleas.

Sometimes it was still hard for her to believe she
was gone. After all, she'd lived with her mother all
her life; her father had died when she was three. Although she had stopped lingering on it long ago, once
in awhile she would still think back, for maybe a minute or two at most, to how she'd ached to go to Vassar
but couldn't bring herself to even consider leaving her
mother. And she'd gotten a good education anyway,
hadn't she? She'd commuted to suburban West Ches-
ter, which had begun as a normal school and become
a university, and over the years she had finally gotten
a master's at Penn. Still...

Of never marrying, she had no regrets at all. There
was really only one young man she'd even considered,
but that too would have involved not only leaving
Mother but the city. Sometimes she did wonder whatever happened to Charles, if he was still alive, what
kind of law he'd come to practice, what kind of family
he had. But as for regrets, none.

She stood up soon and went to the sink with her
dishes, the glass for the orange juice, the cup for her
soft-boiled eggs, the dish for toast, the tea cup of
course, the silver, and washed and dried them carefully. She liked fine things—she used to collect porcelain, much of it during trips abroad with Mother,
and with Mother and Olivia.

Olivia, her only close friend, had died a year before Mother.

Now there was really no one who called her Catherine anymore.

She'd never forget, never, how she'd walked into class the morning after Olivia died, to find them all laughing and yelling—even though they *knew,* they'd just been told that Miss Radcliff had died. Animals, that's all they were, *animals!* And how she'd screamed—even Mrs. Banning in the next room had heard, had come to look silently through the window of the closed door.

A quick glance at the clock over the stove told her she still had half an hour. But it was only a short ride to the school. She opened her old brown leather satchel and took out a thick batch of homework papers. She had to look at them again; she hated to believe they were so bad. Oh, a couple were quite good and a few were absolutely dreadful, but the mass of them were just mediocre—which was bad.

She glanced through them again, hoping she would see some of them differently—but no. It only got her more frustrated, angrier.

Were children always this way? It was hard to remember exactly, but she doubted it. She could never have lasted in teaching this long.

She closed the satchel, then went to the hall closet for her raincoat, which was her all-service coat in cool weather.

If she ever needed anything to renew her sense of accomplishment, it was what was happening with the bicentennial. She was co-chairperson of the Combined Schools Committee—Barwyn High and Elementary, St. Joseph's High and Elementary, and Madsen, a smaller public elementary school so near the outskirts she often had trouble thinking it was really in Barwyn. Their job was to select alumni to be honored. And it was so hard for her, there were so many she'd helped mold: a secretary of commerce, a senator, judges, prominent executives...

She buttoned her coat, then rechecked the house to make sure all the lights and the stove were off. She double-locked the doors, then started to walk to her car, a four-year-old Plymouth. She stopped, with a sharp look of annoyance. She picked up from the lawn a neatly-folded copy of the *Philadelphia Morning Dispatch*.

She was annoyed because she didn't order the paper to be delivered—there were some days she didn't *feel* like reading bad news. And that was all that papers and TV carried these days. What's more, it was as though something were being *forced* on her. It was the second time in the past few weeks this had happened.

STANDING WITH the morning paper that was delivered to his door, Ben soon closed it with a feeling of relief. He'd been afraid there would be a story about Harry being questioned and lying about where he was when Pat was killed. Still, he knew, this wasn't the end of it...what was going to happen was almost inevitable. Once the police learned about the insurance Harry took out on her life—and it had to happen—it wouldn't be long before the first story appeared, before it made the nightly news. And then it would grow. It might start off, as these things often did, with quotes from unidentified "police sources," then reporters would begin digging, would start hounding Harry, with those TV vans parked outside his home, his office.

But that wasn't the scariest part.

What had kept him up half the damn night was what else Harry might be hiding.

He'd really forgotten what a liar Harry could be. As far back as he could remember. The thing was, it was never about anything big—in fact, Harry's cheating on Pat was still as much of a jolt as when he'd first learned of it, still seemed totally out of character. But ever since they were kids that fucking, fucking brother of his would say things he never really meant.

"I'm going out, but I'll be back and I'll take you to the movies." And maybe he would and maybe he wouldn't. Or when they were older: "I'll call you tomorrow," and chances were that if he called at all it would be a week or two later.

Things like that.

And how he always hated it.

And now it scared him.

He took a couple of sips from the bottle of water on his desk, then set it down. Most people—he'd heard this enough about himself—would meet him for the first time and think here's a guy with a kind of broken nose, or maybe it wasn't really a broken nose, and a nice smile and a soft way of speaking who probably never got excited or angry in his life. Only it wasn't true. Though it took a lot to get him angry, when it did happen look out; and when he wanted to do something he wanted to do it fast—churned, in fact. But now, desperate to help Harry, it was as though he were looking on at his brother from the grip of quicksand.

He glanced at his watch: 9:20. He called Harry's

house but the line was busy. He tried twice more, then began going haphazardly through the paper again.

He wondered did Harry change his mind and go to the office after all? He hoped so. But Harry had said last night he wasn't up to it yet.

He tried the house again, kept holding the phone awhile even when it was still busy; kept turning the pages. Then all at once he froze. A headline on the obituary page had caught his attention: PODIATRIST DIES IN FALL. And then the name leading off the story leaped at him. Ellen?

Ellen?

He read the story quickly, dazed. Fell down the basement steps. Husband found her dead.

It was almost impossible to believe—he'd just seen *her, talked* with her, *sat* with her. And the next night *dead!* Her sadness about Pat, George—and now her, too? And in such a stupid way, a stupid accident, her own staircase!

Soon he straightened a little in the chair, a sudden quickening in his chest.

That car, he was thinking of that car. Headlights suddenly on. And the slowing up while the beams inched across them.

His heart was thumping harder.

Pat dead, undoubtedly murdered. George Havers— his wife saying he would never have committed suicide. Now Ellen, another unnatural death. And all within a few weeks.

He sat staring at the paper. Then he looked over at the folder Ellen had given him. It seemed so crazy, what he was thinking, but he opened it quickly. He took out every item about the bicentennial, wondering if George too had been on one of the committees—if this might be something that could possibly link the three of them.

He couldn't find George's name.

But he found himself staring at something else—a photo of Pat and Ellen in the "Neighborhoods" section of the *Dispatch,* along with a short feature about their search into Barwyn's history.

But the caption, he saw to his astonishment, identified each of them as the other. And a quick scan of the story revealed that even their addresses were interchanged.

Slowly, a chill spreading through him, he set the clippings down. Those slow-moving headlights—to make sure, this time, what Ellen really looked like?

Could it be—could it possibly *be*—that Pat had been murdered by mistake?

SIX

IN WEST PHILADELPHIA that morning, some ten miles from Barwyn, Maybelle Collins, an obese African-American woman, was sitting by her living room window overlooking the street. She lived on the second floor of a three-story rowhouse which, like most of its neighbors, had been divided into apartments years ago.

Mrs. Collins had a little transistor radio plugged into her left ear, which she would alternate between religious programs and talk shows. This and just staring out the window were the pleasures of her day.

It was a few minutes after seven when she saw Mr. Harris coming from the house diagonally across the street. He was a thin, slightly-stooped white man, fairly tall, with black hair that was thick at the neck and was in sharp contrast to the pallor of his face. It was the kind of face, the first time she'd seen him, that for some reason reminded her of a certain bony-looking, sad-eyed doctor who'd treated her as a child at the clinic. He must be, she guessed, around thirty-five.

Usually, about eight each morning, he drove off in his junker—she'd heard he worked somewhere as a TV repairman. Right now he was walking toward the corner, probably to the grocery; was wearing a blue nylon windbreaker, open, that looked like it could use a cleaning, though she'd always considered him neat. He'd moved in a few months ago; lived on the first floor, from what she'd heard from the woman who lived on the second.

From the little she'd heard about him, he was a quiet man who never said two words when one, or none, would do. And seemed always willing to do a favor. He'd once come across the street when she was having trouble climbing up the front steps, and he made her wait awhile, then helped her up to the open porch, then waited some more until she gathered her strength and breath to make it to the second floor by herself. And Mr. Jones down the street told her at church about Mr. Harris helping him fix the railing in his backyard. In fact, the only one who ever said anything bad about him—and *that* wasn't really bad, coming from who it did—was that Elviva McKanter, who had three children and no husband and had her belly filled again.

That man, Elviva said—she was afraid he was trying to make up to her Tyrone, and she told Tyrone to stay away. Well, Tyrone was a retarded little fellow who rode around on a three-wheeler bike when all the kids his age had two-wheelers, and none of them had anything to do with him except make fun of him. And the time Elviva was referring to, anyway, Mrs. Collins had seen it for herself. All Mr. Harris did was, he'd been getting out of his car and Tyrone was riding by and his foot got stuck between the pedal and one of the wheels, and Mr. Harris got him free, and after fixing the spokes he was just talking to him when Elviva yelled "Tyrone!" from way up the street.

Mr. Harris was coming back from the corner now. He'd bought a newspaper and something else—he was holding a little bag in his other hand. Her gaze followed him to the door, then she turned away and looked to see what else might be happening on the street.

The man she knew as Mr. Harris had looked perfectly calm, no different from the other times she'd seen him. But his heart had been banging against his ribs as he'd walked to and from the store, and still now as he tossed the bag of potato chips on one of the kitchen chairs. He hadn't wanted to take chances in the store, not only with the owner but with the couple of people waiting in line, and so thought it might be suspicious if he only bought a paper.

He laid the paper flat on the chipped Formica table, almost afraid to go through it.

Dummy!

But he was no dummy! Anyone could have... Couldn't anyone have...?

His breath coming quickly, he began scanning the front page, fast at first and then, with great effort, carefully. No, nothing there. Nor in the whole first section. Nothing in the second section either, at least so far on the first few pages. And then he saw it. Although his heart was still going fast when he finished, it was from relief and exhilaration now.

A fall. An accident. That's what they called it, nothing more. And this time, this time her name was right!

Pushing aside the paper he started to walk out to his car, but paused for a few moments at the wrought-iron-framed mirror on the wall near the door. He told himself, as he'd been telling himself for days now, that this shouldn't bother him. But once again his eyes barely noticed his thin straight nose, his strong chin, but focused immediately on a little fold in the skin that had appeared recently under his right jaw. His fingers went to the loose flesh and he pulled on each side of his throat until it was completely taut.

He kept staring at himself, with a kind of dread to let go: that the old face would come back.

NO MORE THAN five minutes later, as he was driving to work, his mind had shifted completely to something else.

He was late, but as he sat stopped at a red light he kept glancing over at a pay phone on the opposite corner. Right next to it was a parking space.

He tried to resist going to it, wanted to stay on the bit of a high that had managed to return. But, finding he had enough coins, he pulled to the curb the moment the light turned green.

For a few rings he held onto hope—it seemed to be ringing longer than ever. But then: "Hello," that damn recorded voice said, "you've reached four five..."

He lowered the phone. Almost slammed it down.

He'd been getting this for almost two weeks. And suddenly it was as if he'd accomplished nothing. And that it would always be true, if as much as one of them got away.

SEVEN

BEN FIRST THOUGHT of calling George Havers' widow last night. But though he'd known it would be hard to bring himself to do, he was finding it even harder.

It felt eerie in a way that you could ask Information for the listing of a dead man and be given a telephone number—in this case, two numbers: one, George's drugstore, where his body had been found hanging in the basement, the other his residence, both in Northeast Philadelphia. Setting down the phone, Ben kept his hand on it, trying to decide if he really should go through with it, what he would say.

He kept wavering. God, he should be used to making tough calls, to widows, brutalized victims, killers' parents—his work demanded it. But this felt so different. And so when the phone was suddenly ringing under his hand it was as if someone had made up his mind for him.

"Ben. How's it going?" It was Dave Mann, one of his closest friends since high school.

"Good, Dave. Not bad."

Dave, an accountant, had just come back from vacation with his wife and child. He was sorry he couldn't be at Pat's funeral, wanted to know how Harry was, and then just to kibbitz a little before settling down to work.

"So," he said, "It's really off between you and Corinne?"

"Really off." Dave was making it sound as if they'd been engaged. But it was something that had just faded away. Mutually.

"She was a real beauty."

"I know." He was looking at the two phone numbers he'd jotted down, having suddenly decided; was anxious to make the call. But Dave was rambling on, about how he and Emma, you know, weren't going to let him stay single much longer, in fact a friend of Emma's had mentioned she had a girlfriend...

As soon as he hung up Ben picked up the receiver again and began tapping out one of the numbers—the residence first.

A woman answered, her hello quiet, flat. "Yes," she said, "this is Mrs. Havers."

"Mrs. Havers," he said uneasily, "my name's Ben Newman."

"I'm sorry, who?"

"Ben Newman. I knew your husband—I used to live in Barwyn and I went through grammar school and high school with him. And I knew"—he almost said "know," it was so hard to think of her as dead—"Ellen Woods. Packler-Woods."

"Oh, God. Ellen." Her voice broke. "I just heard about her."

"Yes," he said, "I can hardly believe it. I just saw her the night before." There was silence, but he could hear her tremulous breathing. "She's the one who told me about George," he said. "I want you to know how sorry I am."

"I appreciate that." Her voice became stronger. It

seemed to come from her sudden desire to talk about her husband. "You say you went to school together?"

"Yes. Actually all the way back to kindergarten."

"Oh, how nice." She paused, then: "I'm trying to remember George mentioning you."

"I doubt if he would have. We hadn't seen each other since high school." There was silence; she was obviously wondering why he would be calling now. "Mrs. Havers, I want to ask you something." He could feel his tension building again. "Do you know about the bicentennial Barwyn's having?"

"I know they're having one."

"Was George connected with it in any way?"

Again silence. Then she said hesitantly, "I don't know what you mean connected. But he was going to get an award."

He heard her ask why, but for a few moments he was too caught up in the sudden rushing of his blood to answer. Then: "Mrs. Havers, would it be possible for me to see you?"

"Why?"

"I'd like to discuss something with you that Ellen mentioned to me."

"You're starting to scare me, you know."

"I don't mean to," he said quickly. "Please. There's nothing to be scared about."

"Then why can't we do it on the phone?"

"We can, and I will if you really want, but I think it'll be better if we sit down and talk. It can be any-where—a restaurant, a lobby. Anywhere."

There was silence again. "Let me call you back," she said. "Where can I reach you?"

About ten minutes later his phone rang.

"All right," she said, "come to the house. But I need a few hours."

IT WAS ALMOST TWO O'CLOCK when he pulled up to her house, a split-level of brick and frame, separated from similar neighbors by white fencing. A slender, softly attractive young woman came to the door; her face, slightly oval, with large green eyes, was set off by short red hair. She was wearing a trim, gray flannel skirt and a pink cardigan, buttoned just at the bottom. The open throat of her blouse showed a hint of a thin, gold necklace.

No, she wasn't Mrs. Havers—Sharon was upstairs on the phone. "She'll be down in a minute. Please come in."

In the living room she said with a slight smile, "You wouldn't remember me, I'm sure. Nancy Dean? I went to Barwyn?"

He looked at her, frowning slightly, trying to place her in the past. And then as it started to come together, he thought there was no way it could be.

He thought of the little long-haired thing—he'd always thought of her as a kind of thing—with a thin wise-guy smile who Phil Schultz had said, way back in at least the fifth grade, had let him finger her under her skirt behind a billboard. None of them believed it, but soon there were stories from a couple of other kids, all of them cruds. That she let you put it in her mouth, and then that she screwed. She was the first girl he'd ever seen face to face who he knew "did" it, something that had been completely out of his world.

He heard himself say, "Oh, of course," and then the usual, stupid-sounding thing: "It's been a long time."

"God yes."

She'd been left back at least once—it was probably, again, in the fifth grade. It came back to him how it used to work at Barwyn—so barbaric—how, when the kids who were told they were promoted stood up and went in a group to their new teacher's room, the few unfortunates left back used to remain seated. She'd been one of those. So, not only those stories, but she'd been left back—which had made her even more of a thing. He'd never had reason to speak to her, she'd never been in his class again, though he used to see her around, then and in high school, always with the sleazy kids; from maybe the sixth grade on, she always had long, long earrings and the tightest jeans, and her hair tossed.

He just couldn't match that up with this person here.

"You know one of the things I remember about you?" she asked.

His immediate thought was something about being on the wrestling or swimming teams, but she surprised him by saying, "The movie review column you wrote for the paper."

He said, smiling, "Did I send you off to some bad movies?"

"No, not at all." Then, "Sharon called me, asked did I know you. And I remembered that... Look, Sharon should be right down." She seemed a little awkward all at once, as though he hadn't been supposed to know that Sharon had checked on him, that obviously she'd held off seeing him until Nancy was here to make sure who he was. Then she said, a slight quiver in her voice, "George was my cousin."

"I didn't know that. I was so sorry to hear about him. He was such a terrific guy."

"And I knew Ellen," she said, nodding. "I only live a few blocks from her."

"That was a real shocker. I mean I just *saw* her."

"I know. I heard."

Sharon was coming down the stairs now. She was tall and very thin, with frizzy blond hair and bulging eyes. Her hand trembled slightly as she lifted a cigarette to her lips, drew in. She looked for a long moment at Nancy, then at Ben with a little nod. She took another deep pull on the cigarette before grinding it out.

"Shar," Nancy said, "I'm going to be leaving."

"No, please."

She gestured for them to sit down, then looked at Ben from the sofa. "So. Tell me." There was something of defiance in her voice, as if readying herself for bad news.

He rested his elbows on his knees, hands clasped. "The reason I'm here"—this was so hard to do—"is to find out if something Ellen told me is right. And there's no easy way to put it. She said you don't believe George would have committed suicide."

Sharon's eyes immediately became glazed with tears, but her face took on a firmness. "I don't. I never will. But why?"

"This might have nothing to do with George, nothing at all. But did either of you know my sister-in-law, Pat Newman? Her maiden name was Chandler. She was originally from Barwyn."

Sharon shook her head slowly, but Nancy wanted to know where she went to school. When she heard that Pat had gone to Barwyn's other elementary school, Madsen Elementary, and then Barwyn High, she said, "I know she and Ellen were doing something for the bicentennial."

"Yes."

"That's how I knew of her, though I didn't get to know her personally. Yes, poor soul, I heard she died."

"That's how I met Ellen again, at her funeral." He told them about visiting Ellen and walking out of her office and the headlights suddenly coming on, and the reason why, when he learned she'd died, it bolstered his feeling that his sister-in-law might have been killed by mistake. "Then when you told me George was also involved in the bicentennial I had to see you. It could be coincidental, God knows it probably is, but the three of them in the bicentennial die in what, within three weeks?"

Sharon was staring at him in bewilderment. "But I don't see— I mean, all it was, he was getting an award."

"Did he ever say anything about anyone threatening him?"

"No. No. No one could have had anything against George." She pressed her hands against her temples. "I'm so confused. All I know is he wouldn't have done this to me, to our children. There wasn't even a note. They said—they said maybe he was depressed about the Medicaid thing. But he wasn't, really, it didn't even go to the grand jury. Some doctor, some crazy doctor tried to implicate him in some kind of Medicaid fraud, but it was a lie and they didn't even charge him. And anyway he would never leave me like this—I just found out I have lupus. Would he, Nancy? He wasn't the kind."

Nancy, sitting next to her, her face anguished, shook her head.

"All I know," Sharon said, "is he wouldn't. We were even making plans for our anniversary. And he was so happy about this, let me show you."

She went into another room and came back with a framed, laminated section of a newspaper, showing a picture of fourteen former Barwyn High and St. Joseph High athletes who were going to be honored.

"He was so proud of this."

Ben looked at the faces. George's was the only one he recognized. It was a high school picture, showing him in shoulder pads—the rugged blond kid who charmed everyone.

His eyes went over the faces again, then to the date of the paper.

He pulled in a breath.

Pat's and Ellen's picture had been in the *Dispatch,* one of the city's dailies, while George's was in the *Barvyn Reporter,* a neighborhood weekly. And like with Pat and Ellen, it had been published only a couple of weeks before he died.

WHEN HE GOT back home there was a message from his niece to call her. Even her hello, when he returned her call, sounded frantic.

"Uncle Ben, what's happening with Daddy?"

"Why, what's the matter? What happened?"

She started to say something but her grandmother took the phone. "All we know," she said, "is that he's at police headquarters. With a lawyer."

"Are you saying he's been arrested?"

"I don't know what's happening. All I know is he went there with a lawyer."

"How long's it been?"

"It's at least two hours. What is it, did he tell you anything?"

"I don't know anything about this. I'll try to find out. Look," wishing he meant this, "it's nothing, I'm sure. I'm sure they just want some more information. They have to do these things. Now both of you try to stay calm. I'll go over there and get back to you."

He drove to the Police Administration Building, where an officer at the front desk in a Plexiglas enclosure nodded at the mention of Harry's name. "He's still with detectives," he said, gesturing upstairs.

"Can I wait for him there?"

"No. Sorry."

"Can I stay here?"

"If you want."

There was no place to sit and he felt too anxious, too restless anyway. He walked outside but then came back. After about three quarters of an hour he saw Harry approaching with a man carrying a briefcase. When Harry saw him, he drew in his lips, nodding quickly. The three of them stood outside on the front steps.

"They're trying to make a big thing of it," Harry said softly.

His lawyer said, "All right, all right, not here. Go about your life, your work, you hear me? And nothing to no one, you hear?" Harry nodded. "All right," the lawyer said. "I've got to run." He'd driven Harry here, but Ben would take him home. "I'll talk to you tomorrow. But remember."

At first, when they walked outside, Ben didn't notice the two men looking at them from the sidewalk. Then he saw that one was holding a camera.

"Doctor," the other said, walking along with them, "what about this Sally Glennon? What's your relationship with her?" They kept walking. "When did you meet her?" Then, "Is it true you recently took out a life insurance policy on your wife?"

Ben wanted to take a swing at him, but kept walking. He could hear the whirring sounds of the camera. And now the photographer was in front of them, walking backward and snapping away. He couldn't seem to get enough pictures.

EIGHT

As THEY NEARED his car, Ben said without looking at Harry, "Don't start walking fast, keep your head up, don't give them what they want." Harry slid in quickly and Ben, with a look over at them, a hard look, went to the driver's side.

"Harry, keep your head the hell up," and Harry even deliberately turned to look at them as Ben drove off. But then when Ben glanced over at him he saw him sag; his face was grayish.

"I...did something," Harry said weakly. "Shaster didn't want me to but I wanted to do it. I took a lie detector test." Ben looked at him, startled. "And they said it was inconclusive. Inconclusive."

Ben wanted to pull to the curb but there were no spots.

"He told me don't do it, you don't know these machines, you don't know how you'll react, you don't have to do it. And 'inconclusive.' I should have listened. I was too nervous, I was too upset."

Ben felt the anger boiling up in him, but fought not to show it; had to try to keep giving him support. "All right, so you did it. It didn't really hurt you."

"I was sure that would be the end of it. The end of it. And then those reporters, I didn't expect reporters."

"Fuck 'em. You've got to just fuck 'em."

"I"—Harry turned to him—"Ben, I didn't do anything. You know that, don't you?"

And this time he did pull over. He braked the car but kept the motor running. "Harry, stop that. You hear me? I don't want to hear it again. I never want to hear it again."

"I just wanted you to know."

"Well, cut it out. Now I want to tell you something I've learned. And I'm going to the police with it."

He told him about the possible mix-up between Pat and Ellen, and how George Havers, too, had been connected with the bicentennial. But afterward, when he expected some sort of reaction, Harry just looked at him without expression. Then he slowly stared down at his lap. It was as though what he'd heard was meaningless. That Ben had become...just his kid brother again.

"Look," he said, without looking up, "just drop me off at the house and you go on. It's going to be coming out, so I've got to tell Joannie and—and Pat's mother."

BEN EXPECTED IT on the front page the next morning, but the *Dispatch* ran it on the fourth page. There was a picture of Harry and him walking to the car—Harry, goddamn it, his head bent. The caption read: *Harry Newman, MD (right), leaving the Police Administration Building with an unidentified companion.* The story actually took up little more space than the picture.

CARDIOLOGIST QUESTIONED
IN WIFE'S DEATH

Harry Newman, MD, 39, a prominent Chestnut Hill cardiologist, underwent what detectives de-

scribe as routine questioning in the mysterious
death of his wife, Patricia, on the night of April
21.

Mrs. Newman, also 39, was found dead, fully
clothed, in the swimming pool of their home at
31 Wilhelm Street. According to the medical ex-
aminer, the victim had suffered severe injuries to
her forehead, but the actual cause of death was
drowning.

Dr. Newman, who was accompanied by an at-
torney...

The story said that Harry had come in "voluntar-
ily" and was described by police as having been "co-
operative." It went into some of Harry's and Pat's
background, but said nothing about Sally Glennon,
nothing about the lie detector test, nothing about insurance.

The paper, Ben knew, was obviously playing it safe
until there was more evidence or, of course, charges
were filed. But this was the start he had been afraid
of—the first step toward the front page.

And, he couldn't help thinking, this item would be
something he'd clip out if he were looking on this as
a true-detective writer. He would date it and put it in
a manila envelope and label it NEWMAN, hoping
he'd be filling it up.

THE MAN CALLED HARRIS made sure his car was
locked, then walked to his door in his slightly stooped
way. He looked in his mailbox in the vestibule, even
though no one knew his address but the boss.

In the apartment—he'd rented it furnished—he left

his windbreaker on; it was still a little cool out and he was going out again, to the grocery store. It was more expensive than the supermarket but he hated the crowds there, the lines. All he wanted, anyway, was some baloney; he had white bread left over and some pickles and the potato chips.

He went into the bathroom and washed his face after a long look and a pull at the skin, then ran his wet hands over his combed-back hair.

He'd fixed seven sets today, all in the houses; didn't have to bring a single one back to the shop, which the boss—he hated even thinking that word, he'd *been* a boss—which the boss didn't like. He liked you to bring back all of them if you could. You could often charge more in the shop. And the fact was, today the companies deliberately made them where you had to reorder the whole guts.

When he'd worked with Papa, he always, always, always fixed every set he could in people's homes. And it was like it was his own shop, there was no difference. He used to have two guys working under him, and after awhile Papa never even worked at the bench; he'd handle the books and the customers. Papa'd been so good with customers, especially when there was a blowup: he could calm people down when he himself was this close to throwing them out or—he still didn't know how this never happened—or hitting them or something.

HARRIS ELECTRONICS. The sign actually said it twice, for it had been a corner store with two windows.

But he soon shut out these images, for they only made him sad. And he thought of how the time was almost here, right here, when he'd have that bitch right in front of him.

"Miss Cassaway," he would greet her, with a big smile. No. Noo. Not that at all. "Miss Cass-a-way," he'd say.

A LITTLE LATER, leaving the house to go to the store, he saw Tyrone up the street, staring at him. He wanted to wave but was afraid it would bring out his mother.

Like to kill that mother. All he had wanted to do was fix his bike.

He'd calmed down pretty much by the time he got to the store. He asked the young black girl behind the counter for half a quarter pound of baloney.

She said, "You say what?"

"Half a quarter." Almost yelled it. Why did people always make you feel you have to explain everything?

Afterward, at the cash register, he remembered wanting a newspaper and took one of the two morning papers remaining on the rack. He walked back with it under his arm.

In the apartment he started to make a sandwich but then stopped. Ever since lunch he'd been tempted to try making the call again but had managed to hold off. He'd called twice this morning but got so frustrated he swore he wouldn't try again until tomorrow—and then had given it an arbitrary time of eight o'clock tonight.

But he was weakening.

He went to the phone and dialed her number quickly.

"You have reached four five—"

He hung up fast, not wanting to hear more of that recorded voice. And now he was furious at himself, as he'd known he would be.

He waited a while, then finished making the baloney

sandwich. He sat down with it, slowly turning the pages of the paper as he chewed.

At first it was only a picture of two guys. But then he saw the name Harry Newman, MD, and he started to read the story. Then his eyes went back to the face of the fellow without a name.

He stared at it.

Hadn't it been Newman? Hadn't his name been Newman too?

He kept staring at the face, but the features stayed the same, familiar. But then gradually, his excitement building, those features began to change into a kid's face, *that* kid's face. Ben Newman's face.

How could he ever have forgotten him?

NINE

THE FOLLOWING AFTERNOON Ben received a packet containing a batch of newspaper clippings, black-and-white photos, and a tape recording. They were from a reporter in a town in Western Pennsylvania, some two hundred and seventy miles away, whom Ben had retained to do the legwork on a case there. He did this now and then, with his editor's okay, when he couldn't personally research an out-of-town story.

This was the case of a young barmaid, whose body had been found by two deer hunters. She had been beaten and strangled by a volunteer fireman.

Ben, his mind focused, went through the clippings and photos, then listened to the tape, making notes on a yellow legal pad. It was an interview of the lead investigator.

From the time he'd first started doing these stories, Ben had made up his mind about how he'd approach them. It was so easy to cheat on them, to make up wild action and phony suspects and clues, but once he'd found that he had the knack of writing them he'd promised himself he would do them honestly and the best he could. And it had to do with more than being honest. Though using these stories as a means to an end, to making it one day with books and solid articles, he would never hurt himself as a writer this way.

He was almost through the tape when his phone rang. He took it on the first ring, then sat up a little straighter, surprised to hear it was Sharon Havers' red-haired friend, Nancy Dean.

He wondered how she'd gotten his number, which was unlisted, then quickly remembered that he had given it to Sharon. He'd had it unlisted during the hassle to get Jerry Tomavich cleared and out of prison, when he'd gotten so many off-the-wall calls.

"Do you have a minute?" she asked.

"Not a minute. All the time in the world."

"I just remembered something which probably doesn't have anything to do with any of this, but I thought you might like to know since it concerned the bicentennial. About five, six months ago, there was some kind of problem, some kind of fighting going on. I really don't know the details, but I assumed it blew over. At least I never heard any more about it. I own a secretarial service in Barwyn and do some work for the bicentennial. I learned about the problem when the board had me send out a mailing to members of the committees. I don't have a copy, but I remember it saying that the 'dissidents'—I remember that word very well—anyway, that they were just trying to be disruptive, but it could be resolved. And that's really the last I heard of it."

"Do you know who any of these people are?"

"No, I heard a couple of names once, but they didn't mean anything to me."

"Can you suggest someone I could talk to?"

She thought, then, "I really don't know who'd be best, who'd even talk to you about it. But I'll tell you what. If you want a list of the members, they're on the stationery; there're about twenty-five. If you'd like I could mail it or fax it."

He looked at his watch. It was after four. He said, "Would it be okay if I picked it up? Maybe you could tell me something about some of them. And frankly I wouldn't mind getting out of here for a while."

"Sure."

HER HOME WAS only three blocks from the high school—a speckled-stone twin with an open porch. A small white wooden sign by the door said: DEAN SECRETARIAL SERVICES, and underneath: PHOTOCOPYING & FAXING.

She must have heard him park or walk up the steps, because she opened the door before he could ring the bell. "Hi." She smiled slightly. She wore a white blouse, the sleeves pushed up, and a thin-belted khaki skirt. He hadn't remembered quite how short her hair was.

He said, "I really appreciate your calling."

"As I said," closing the door, "I don't know what this could have to do with... I doubt anything. But it's the only thing I can think of involving the bicentennial."

He looked around. "You've got quite a setup here."

There were a couple of desks in what used to be a living room, one with a computer, one with an electric typewriter, and at the far end were file cabinets, a copy machine and a fax.

"I'm thinking about moving," she said. "My next door neighbor has started giving me a rough time, and I don't want to stay here anyway."

"I guess that takes care of you two walking together in the bicentennial parade."

She laughed. "I would hope so."

"And you live here, right?"

"Oh yeah. It's the house where I grew up. I moved back with my mother after my divorce. She was a widow. She died last year."

He looked around at the desks again, then at her with a smile. "You don't just run from one to the other, do you?"

She smiled back. "Sometimes, but I have a full-time employee and one who works part-time, though it's gotten so busy I'm probably going to have to take on another part-timer. If anyone told me even three years ago I'd be doing this kind of work, I'd have said they were crazy. I *hated* typing. And I was perfectly terrible at it in school. But then again I was perfectly terrible at everything."

"Come on. Nobody's perfect at anything, even being terrible."

She laughed. "Well, almost. Anyway," she said, going to one of the desks, "let me show you."

She handed him a piece of stationery with the Barwyn bicentennial logo and a column of names running down one side. He scanned the names quickly, stopping at Pat's and Ellen's listed above their committee. She sensed what he was looking at.

"I was looking at that too," she said.

He looked at her, then back at the other names, carefully this time. And a name he'd somehow overlooked, though it was second from the top as co-director, riveted him. Daniel Haupt.

He and Danny, he explained, had been very, very close as kids.

"You know, he's been running the hardware store since his father died," she said.

"Yes, I heard. I'm going to call him." They began to drift slowly to the door. "Tell me," he said, "how's Sharon?"

"Oh, confused."

"I probably made it worse for her, didn't I?"

"No." She shook her head quickly. "No one could make it worse than what she's been doing to herself."

He opened the door, paused, looked at her. He'd been thinking of this for the past few moments, wanted to ask but was hesitant for some reason; didn't want to embarrass her or himself. "I was just wondering. Would you like to have dinner with me?" He couldn't tell from her look whether she was simply surprised or just uncertain. "I wish you would," he said.

She kept looking at him with that same expression, but her face had reddened slightly. "That would be nice," she said.

SHE SUGGESTED a place a few blocks away, which she said didn't look like much but the food was quite good. From the outside it looked like an ordinary neighborhood taproom, and half of it was, but past the long bar, through an archway, was a softly-lighted restaurant, with booths and open, tablecloth-covered tables. Though the bar was fairly crowded, this room was almost empty.

He asked, "Would you like something to drink?"

"Maybe a chablis." After the waitress left with their order she immediately opened the menu.

He looked at her. She had long lashes and there were a few freckles on her cheeks he hadn't noticed before. She didn't look up until their drinks came. He raised his glass toward her, then she raised hers, a little awkwardly.

"Cheers," he said. "That's a little toast I read about in a book."

She smiled and they both took a sip.

"Know what you want to eat?" he asked.

"I think so." She looked back at the menu.

He asked, his eyes on the menu, "How's their Italian food?"

"I think very good. Their new chef's Italian and I think he's particularly good."

She ordered a crab cake platter, he mussels marinara and linguini. After the waitress took away the menus, Nancy looked at him.

She was curious about his work, where he went to school, where he'd been all these years, asked him a few questions, then said, "Can you think of anything dumber than what I did? I hate to admit it, but like an idiot I dropped out of school in the twelfth grade—the *twelfth* grade, can you imagine? My marks were okay, I would have graduated, but then I met this fellow and he said let's get married and we just ran off. Second month of the twelfth grade. I can't believe it to this day."

The marriage lasted four years. No children.

"It's strange," she said. "My father was the quietest, mildest man you could meet. And I guess—no, I know—I didn't like him for it. Hated him for it sometimes. I mean, the things my mother would do— even boyfriends. And he didn't do anything about it. A lot of my life, I think, I wanted to get back at him. I don't know. And when I got married, it was to the exact opposite. Drank—my father rarely did. And always yelling. And hit, oh, he was a good hitter. Finally"—she looked up with a smile, but there was a sadness to it—"I thought, Enough, I'm going to make it on my own. I didn't move right back here—my mother was the last person I wanted to live with, and Barwyn was the last place I really wanted to be. I took a little place, I waitressed, I worked in a department store. Then I started this business. Then my mother got sick and darn near pleaded with me to move back with her. And in a way I'm glad I did. I made a kind of peace with her. But now I want out of the house, out of Barwyn.''

"You deserve a lot of credit for what you've done."

She smiled, but a little sadly. "Well, I finally did get my diploma a few years ago. An equivalency diploma."

"Good. Great."

She looked at him. "You *are* nice," she said with a smile. "You make it sound like Harvard."

PARKED IN FRONT of her house, the motor running, he said, "I'll talk to you after I call Dan. I'll let you know what he has to say."

"Please. Look, thanks so much for dinner."

"You kidding? Thank you."

He slid out and walked around. By that time she was out, too. He walked with her up the steps to her porch. He watched as she rooted around in her handbag for her key, then unlocked the door. She turned with a brief smile. "Thanks again. Goodnight."

"Goodnight."

Driving away he became aware, as though for the first time, of how much he'd talked, how much he'd enjoyed hearing her talk, just being with her. It was only as he approached his apartment building that the full weight of his brother's problems was back.

TEN

BEN GOT A LETTER the next day from his agent, who had handled the sale of his book, explaining that he had been unable to get a go-ahead from *Vanity Fair* on an article Ben had proposed. He would try other magazines, he assured him, but this had seemed like the natural market for it.

Ben tossed it on his desk: he was disappointed, of course, but he'd half expected that it wasn't quite for them. He sat there thinking about it awhile, then mentally turned it off, and drew the phone to him. Although still uneasy about what he was going to do, he called Detective McGlynn.

"Bill McGlynn here."

"Hi, this is Ben Newman. How are you?"

"Okay. Just about the same complaints as yesterday. What can I do for you?"

"I want to see you, but I'd like it to be someplace where we can talk privately."

"No problem, kid. Come on down."

MCGLYNN, A MAN of fifty-two whose close-cropped gray hair somehow made him look younger, took him into an office and closed the door. He leaned back against the front of the desk.

Ben, trying to appear calm, asked, "Are you familiar with the Patricia Newman case in Chestnut Hill? The woman found dead in her swimming pool?"

"Yeah. It's not mine, but I'm familiar with it."

"She was my sister-in-law. Her husband's my brother."

McGlynn's eyebrows lifted slightly. "Oh. Newman. Yeah."

"Bill, there are some things I think the police ought to know. But I don't know if you'd prefer me to go to someone else with it or tell you."

"Well, the main guy who's handling it isn't in right now, but if you want, you can tell me. I'll see he gets it."

The detective's face was expressionless and never changed as Ben went through the whole story. Then he frowned thoughtfully. "That car when you were with the podiatry lady, did you get the license number?"

"No. I never thought to. I couldn't even tell you the make."

"Let me make sure I got this completely straight. Your sister-in-law, you feel, might have been killed because she was mistaken for this Ellen Packler-Woods."

"As I said, they were identified as each other in the paper. But what I've really begun to wonder is if the three deaths aren't actually connected with the bicentennial. It's such a big coincidence if they aren't. Anyway, I just want to pass it along."

McGlynn kept looking at him, then took out a notebook and made some notes. Then he held it down at his side. "How's your brother doing?"

It sounded so friendly, so concerned, that it was a moment before Ben realized it could be a trick, that he could be trying to trap him into making some damning comment.

"He's doing okay, considering. He'll be fine."

"Well, kid, just know I'm here. Feel free to come to me with anything. Anything. Remember that, okay?"

"I appreciate that, Bill. Thanks."

"Anything. I mean it."

"I know you do."

McGlynn, his eyes still on him, nodded slightly.

"But he's really doing fine," Ben repeated. And all this time, he was sure, McGlynn had to be thinking of things he must have heard, of Sally Glennon and the insurance and Harry lying about where he was that night, and the absence of any other motive but perhaps a husband's fury or greed.

Here was a guy, he reflected as he left, he'd done such great things with, like that time—he could pick out so many—when McGlynn had him along on a manhunt and they grabbed the killer as he was trying to squeeze himself up into a chimney. Or when they got a laugh in that taproom where McGlynn, after walking with him along the bar while he searched out faces, pointed out it was such a thieves' den they even chained the cigarette machine to the wall so no one would steal it.

And a chasm, as he'd feared, had not only opened between them but it probably couldn't be wider.

HE STOPPED ON the way back to his apartment to call Danny Haupt, at his store. After not seeing him for years, it felt a little goofy to be suddenly calling him from the street. But he couldn't hold off.

"Dan." He turned his back to the few cars going by. "Someone from your past. Ben Newman."

There was just a moment's hesitation. "Ben," and he could picture the big smile. No matter what Danny said, no matter how serious, it was almost always with a smile. "Hey, it's good to hear from you."

They didn't spend a lot of time talking about how long it had been or why they hadn't been in touch. They were immediately caught up in talking with each other. Danny had heard about Ben publishing a book, wanted to know about his mother and father. Danny's widowed mother was still living in Barwyn, with her sister. Yeah, he was married, had a little girl. You? No?

"Danny, I'd like to see you. If at all possible, today. You happen to be free any time?"

"Sure. Name it."

"How about like now?"

"Sure thing. Great."

Danny's grandfather—maybe his great-grandfather—had started Haupt's Hardware and Paints store. It stood on the same corner of Barwyn's busy main shopping street where it had been founded; it had been a single store when Ben lived here, but they'd expanded into the adjoining building. Walking in, he looked around at the several faces for one he could pick out as Danny's. But the clerk who approached him said Mr. Haupt was in the office, he would get him.

Ben drifted along one of the aisles, remembering the times he used to come here with Danny, sometimes on their way to a Saturday movie when Danny had to pick up some money. It had always been such a marvelous place, particularly since it also carried toys.

And Danny—Ben had been thinking of this on the drive here, that he didn't think there could be any friend he'd ever love more than Danny in those years; no times sweeter than playing in the woods near the Catholic church and the hours they spent in the "bunk" they'd made out of a shed under Ben's house. And no day happier than when he'd gotten into Danny's class.

He'd been a grade behind Danny, and one day the teacher in second or third grade gave him a sealed envelope to take home. He couldn't imagine what he'd done, except maybe he needed more shots or something terrible like that, but he would never have thought to open it. Then when he got home his mother sliced it open with a knife, frowned and then with a wide smile said, "You're skipping a grade."

He remembered running over to Danny's, just a few houses down the street, but no one was home; and Danny was already gone the next morning when he ran over there to walk with him to school. He could still see Danny's big-eyed look in the back of the classroom as he walked in.

It was hard to remember exactly why they'd drifted apart. Just different interests and then different friends, beginning in high school.

Danny was walking toward him now, in a long-sleeve shirt and tie—heavier, but no mistaking Danny. The first thing Ben really took in was the same big smile; but just about everything else was the same too: the hair, wheat-colored and curly, the pointy face, with a few little scars where there'd been acne.

"Hey." Danny took his hand in both of his and held on hard. "You look good."

"You do too, lad."

In his office Danny rolled a chair from behind his desk so he could sit closer to Ben. Still grinning, he looked at him, arms folded on his chest and a leg crossed on his knee.

"It's great seeing you," he said. "Great seeing you." Then after a few more moments of catching up with each other, "I don't know whether you heard about it, but my brother Harry's wife died. Patricia?"

Danny clamped a hand on his forehead. "Of course I knew. How could it have slipped my mind? She's the one told me you wrote a book. I'm damn sorry. So damn sorry. Tell me, how's Harry?"

"It's been pretty rough."

Then Danny said he didn't know if Ben remembered her, but they had another tragedy around here. "Ellen Packler? She became Ellen Packler-Woods? Do you remember Ellen?"

"Sure. And the thing I can't get over is I saw her the night before it happened." As Danny frowned, Ben said, "And do you know about George Havers dying? I imagine you do."

Nodding, Danny slowly lowered his crossed leg, though his arms remained folded. The smile was gone.

"All this is really what I want to talk to you about," Ben said.

Danny's frown deepened as Ben began, starting with Pat's death, moving on to George's wife denying that he would have ever committed suicide, and then to Ellen and the headlights. After a pause, and with Danny looking at him puzzled, Ben said, "I think it's an awful coincidence that three people involved in the bicentennial die within a few weeks of each other. And they're not natural deaths. Furthermore, each of their pictures was in the paper a short time before they died—Pat and Ellen in the *Dispatch*, George in *The Reporter* here.''

Dan—somehow it was no longer Danny—was looking at him gravely, but a little strangely too.

''Dan, can I ask you something?''

''Sure. Of course.''

''I've heard there was some kind of squabble about the bicentennial. About six months ago. If you don't want to tell me what it was about, don't. But what I want to know is do you think it could possibly fit in?''

Dan had to think. Then he said, ''Oh. That. You know who was behind that, don't you? Remember Wild Man Nevon?''

Of course. One of their eighth grade teachers. Home room and social studies. He'd been a great guy, never really deserved ''Wild Man,'' but that's what passed from class to class. He would pace, he'd sit with a foot up on his desk, he'd argue, even let the kids yell once in awhile, hushing them up only when he thought it might bring the principal.

''He's at the high school now,'' Dan said. ''Anyway, he had some bug up his ass for awhile. Him and some of the others, but he was pretty much the spokesman. But it all passed. Believe me, there was nothing to it. Naah,'' he said, shaking his head and smiling again. ''In fact, speaking of Nevon,'' he went on, grinning, ''remember that time he plunked Cookie—remember Cookie?—on the head with a wad of paper to get his attention? A real nutty guy. I think he was a Red, probably still is for all I know.''

This led him to other reminiscences about Nevon, then about a few of the other kids, a couple of whom still lived in Barwyn, including Cookie. ''Believe it or not, he turned out to be a nice guy. He used to be such a *pain*. He's got an auto repair shop a few blocks away. But look," he said then, "that little thing about the bicentennial..." He shook his head. "It was nothing. Believe me." Then he smiled and said, "I'm afraid we aren't very exciting around here. I don't know if you're thinking of one, but we wouldn't make much of a book."

ELEVEN

NAAH, DANNY HAD SAID. *It was nothing. Believe me.*

He should let it rest at that. Danny would know if whatever had happened had been anything that could possibly lead to murder, to *murders*. And, God, he had his own work to do!

But it was like a tiny splinter under his fingernail.

If this didn't involve Nevon, he'd probably find it a lot easier to drop. But Ben remembered the guy fondly, as someone easy-going and completely fair, though a little weird. So there was no tension at the thought of calling him, though it did feel a little strange, the idea of going back and talking as an adult with one of your grammar school teachers.

He didn't want to bother him at school, though, where he probably was at this hour; thought it best he leave a message at his house to call him at the apartment. But he didn't remember his first name until he looked in the phone book. Wayne.

Way-un, some of the wise-guys used to call to him on the street. And he'd always wave and smile.

After he asked the woman who answered the phone if he had the right Nevon, she said, "Yes, that's right, this is Mr. Nevon's home—he teaches at the high school."

"Could I leave him a message?"

"Yes, though I probably won't be speaking to him before three. I'm picking him up then and we're going out of town to visit our daughter for a few days."

Ben said, "Do you think I can reach him at school?"

"You can leave a message in the office but sometimes he forgets to look in his box."

"Well, would you give him this message when you see him? This is Ben Newman. I had Mr. Nevon in eighth grade. Please ask him if there's any chance I can see him for a few minutes today. I won't take much of his time. Tell him it's about the bicentennial. I just want to ask him something about it."

Mrs. Nevon called back in a little more than an hour. Her husband had just happened to call her regarding the trip.

"He asked me to ask you one thing," she said. "Are you a writer?"

"Yes."

"Okay. He said get there at two. He's had a little bit of an early day. Go to the principal's office. They'll know where he is."

A SECURITY GUARD, or maybe a teacher, dressed in a dark suit stood inside the main entrance. He'd been given Ben's name, and he asked did he know where the principal's office was.

Ben had never considered not knowing, but damn if he hadn't forgotten. The man told him the way. Ben walked along the quiet corridors—the kids were still in class, just a few drifted by. He'd thought the school would seem small, but it seemed as vast as it had his first day here, perhaps even more so because of the emptiness of the halls.

He was amazed at how much he'd forgotten: where the stairs were, the elevators, the huge glass case with trophies. The lockers in the hall—he would have forgotten about them too if it hadn't been for a few movies he'd seen. The only lockers he really remembered would be downstairs next to the gym. And thinking of that he remembered Willard and how the first time they'd undressed, he stood naked facing a wall until someone turned him around and he had this hard-on.

Poor Willard.

The woman who came to the counter in the office didn't know of his visit, but the young woman she spoke to did. He'd find Mr. Nevon in room 205.

The door was open, the seats empty, and Mr. Nevon was sitting at the desk, right foot up against a drawer and chair tilted back slightly. He turned.

He'd hardly changed. He had the same very thick black hair, now with a few traces of gray. He'd always looked as if he could use a shave, and he still did. Ben remembered the mole near his chin, even remembered wondering how he shaved over it.

"Yes," Nevon said; and with just that word, there was the same gravelly voice. He let his chair go down. He reached up his hand and Ben took it. "Bring over a chair." Ben slid one over, an arm-desk. "The eighth grade," Nevon reflected, staring at him. "Christ, I'm getting ancient."

Ben smiled. It was actually good seeing him again. "I was just thinking," he said, "you've gotten younger. I must have thought you were at least fifty then."

"Let's see. When I left elementary to come here I was twenty-seven."

Twenty-seven? It was hard to believe Wild Man Nevon had been four years younger than he himself was now.

"So," Nevon said, tilting his chair back again, "you're a writer. I know because you got a write-up in the school paper a few months ago."

Ben hadn't seen the story, though someone from the paper had sent him a list of questions to answer.

"I sort of remembered you—you were a pretty bright, quiet kid, unless"—he flickered a smile—"I got the wrong kid. Then a few weeks later they ran a whole list of names of famous graduates. And I'm sure I saw yours."

"Really?"

"Really. I only lie about important things." Ben had forgotten how expertly he could needle you. "Don't you know that in some circles you're a little bit famous? Aren't you in the bicentennial?"

"I'm afraid not."

"Well, maybe you'll make— What comes after a bicentennial? So," he said, letting the chair down again, "what's on your mind? My wife says it's something about the shindig. I need a good story for my friends, I was hoping you wanted me to change your mark."

Ben smiled. Then he said, "Look, what I'm going to say will probably sound crazy, and the odds are it is. But what I hope you'll give it some thought. Have you heard about the deaths of my sister-in-law, Pat Newman, and Ellen Packler-Woods and George Havers?"

"Yeah, I heard about Ellen and George. I remember them. Can't say as I've heard of your sister-in-law."

Nevon looked at him curiously as Ben told him why he was here. "I'm really grabbing at things. I don't know if any of this has anything to do with the bicentennial. But I heard there was a big argument of some kind and I thought, maybe, you know, it was something that might fit in.''

''Well, let me ask you: why're you here and not at the gendarmes?''

''I've gone to them, to someone I know. But frankly I don't think I got anywhere. I'm trying to see if maybe I can give them something more.''

''Let me tell you a little about myself and then you'll know how I got involved. Let's start way back. Do you know how I got out of the elementary school? Strike that—got kicked out? Kicked out, thank God. Because I believed that a social studies teacher should be able to rip into some of our country's policies without a lot of parents jumping up and down saying 'he's a Red.' And marks. I believed if you failed you failed, you didn't graduate. I was actually tough, if you remember. I let the kids yell their balls off in class if I thought they were striving for a point or we were having fun together—but not just to yell. I wouldn't put up with that. But I got all this flack about 'You don't discipline your class,' crap like that. Anyway, they transferred me here. And I love it. I finally had a variety of people to teach. A lot more Jews, even a lot more Catholics. And finally, thank God, the Koreans, Hispanics, the blacks. And I don't have trouble with anyone.

''Of course,'' he said, after a pause, ''I don't teach social studies anymore. They wouldn't let me near that, or history, or anything where I could shoot my mouth off. Math—Jesus, my worst subject. But I learned—I finally got ahead of the kids. I have a family, I told myself if they want me to teach math I'll teach math. And like I told my wife. Honest to God I said, 'Honey, if they want me to shit purple I'm gonna shit purple.' And that's what I've been doing. But this bicentennial thing, it did get the old blood going. What happened is that a number of people got upset because a few of the old families were running the entire thing, had named the committees, had pretty much set up the whole program. But hey, what am I saying?'' Nevon interrupted himself. ''You're probably one of the old families.''

''You kidding?''

''Well, I knew there was something nice about you. Anyway, when I found we were only causing a tumult, when it only became aggravation to me, I decided the hell with it. But we did some good, we got a lot more ethnics into the planning. Anyway''—he smiled— ''I'm right back to shitting purple again.''

Ben was waiting for him to go on, but he didn't. ''Is there anything, anyone, you can think of who might fit in with this?''

Nevon thought, then shook his head. ''No, but I'll tell you what, I'll think about it. Okay?''

''I can't ask for more.''

Nevon, looking at him, slapped his thighs and stood up. Ben followed.

''Meanwhile,'' Nevon said, extending his hand, ''maybe we'll all be in one of your books.''

Unlike Danny, he apparently thought they would make a good one.

WHEN BEN GOT BACK to his apartment, he found that one of the messages on his answering machine was from a Lieutenant Gowan, of the Philadelphia police, asking him to call back. He called the number, frowning. He had a vague feeling of dislike for the name. There'd been only one Gowan he'd known, long ago. And he hadn't known he'd become a cop.

"Gowan here." Brusque—but at Ben's name, the voice immediately became softer, friendly.

"I was wondering if I could talk to you for a few minutes," Ben said. "I wondered if we could meet somewhere."

"Can you tell me what it's about?"

Ben wondered if McGlynn had contacted him with the information he'd given him. "I want to run a theory by you I have about some of the deaths that have been happening around here."

"Okay, sure. I ran into Dan Haupt and he passed along some of your concerns about the bicentennial. What if I stop by your place?"

Putting down the phone Ben had no doubt now who Gowan was. He'd been a couple of grades higher than him and Dan, a bully son of a bitch who'd been sort of a big shot in school, especially in elementary, because his father was commissioner of police at the time, was always in the newspapers and on TV.

He could still feel some of his old hatred—and then a lot of it when he let one incident in particular come back, maybe in the fourth grade, when he'd been walking home from school and Gowan grabbed his books for no reason and threw them up into the wind. And how, after chasing after all those loose papers, Ben had stared, on fire, at him and the other older kids laughing with him, and then did what he'd been absolutely crazy to do—he jumped on him, grabbed his hair and swung him to the ground. He would have bitten his goddamn ear off, would have pulled out a fistful of hair, if they hadn't dragged him off.

But that wasn't the worst. Gowan, after getting up, grinned at him and then started rubbing his thumb and forefinger together, saying, "Money, money, Abie like money?"

At first Ben hadn't known what he meant.

"Money, money," and those fingers.

Then all at once he knew, and he struggled and twisted to get at him again, but someone threw him down and Gowan and his buddies walked off, Gowan looking over his shoulder at him with a grin.

But though once in awhile after that Gowan would look at him with a twisted little grin, he never did bother him again.

GOWAN'S VOICE came over the intercom about an hour later and Ben buzzed him in. He had the same strong good looks, with golden-red hair, that he'd always had and always seemed aware of.

"How's it goin'?" Gowan asked, smiling. They shook hands.

It seemed obvious Gowan remembered him too. And why not?

They took chairs by the picture windows. Gowan smiled as he settled in. There was, Ben saw, something vaguely John Kennedy-ish about him. And with that touch of Kennedy features, he had the look of a man who was going straight up, perhaps to his father's old job. He was even dressed in a way that more than suggested it. He was wearing a sports jacket, a button-down shirt, a Liberty tie, and what appeared to be, from the glimpse Ben got of it under the cuff and cuff-links, an expensive watch. And he seemed so friendly that Ben felt himself letting go of most of the hate. It was stupid, it was so long ago, they'd been kids.

"Like I told you," Gowan said, "I ran into Dan and he told me. Anyway, I want you to know I knew Ellen Woods and her husband. I still live in Barwyn, you know. I'm not in Homicide, I'm in Internal Affairs, but after Ellen's death I checked up on it, talked to a couple of the boys, and it *was* an accident. I mean, there was absolutely nothing to indicate it was anything else. It wasn't a robbery. And I don't think she ever made an enemy in her life; she had a good marriage. You know? And the injuries fit in with that kind of fall—a wicked set of stairs, you'd think they'd have them carpeted. Anyway, I just wanted you to know from the horse's mouth."

Ben said, "I assume you know about the car when we came outside. It was like someone wanted to get a good look at us. At her."

Gowan nodded. "Look," he said, and in it was a touch of hey, come *on*. "I don't know anything about your sister-in-law's murder or George Havers' suicide. I don't know. But I do know about Ellen, I *really* know about Ellen. Okay?"

Ben said nothing. Just looked at him.

"Well…" Gowan smiled. It was a warm smile. "You going to take part in the big celebration this Fall?"

"Only if they let me wear a funny hat."

Gowan smiled. "It's gonna be something."

"So I hear."

Gowan stood up slowly. "You know," he said, "the reason I wanted to tell you in person is really a selfish one, I guess. I don't want any of these people hurt. I've lived here forever, my mom and dad lived here forever, and I'd like those people to have their celebration without any rain on it."

Ben looked at him curiously. "You know, I'm not out to hurt anyone. And I'm from Barwyn too, remember?"

Gowan seemed a little startled. "Hey, I'm sorry, I didn't mean it the way it sounded."

"I know." Ben held out his hand. "Take it easy."

"You too."

Ben watched him walk off.

No way had Danny simply run into him: Danny'd called him to have him try to put an end to it. Danny, who used to "hate" Gowan, too.

It was a little weird, this feeling. Pat was dead, with Harry under suspicion, and Ellen and George were dead, and God only knew if anyone else was next. But all he was thinking of at this moment, he was aware, was Danny. It was almost as if he'd sat with him under the trees again or in one of their bedrooms, and had shared a confidence with him. And Danny had broken and belittled it.

TWELVE

"EVENIN', MR. HARRIS."

He turned, startled, then saw that it was only that fat lady from across the street. He lifted his hand slightly and now she was hoisting herself up the front steps with the help of the iron railing. He kept walking toward the corner.

He was already tense enough without having his name called out in the dark.

As he walked he took all his change out of his pocket and counted it in his palm. He went to the open phone across the street from the grocery store—didn't want to use his own phone, it might be traced. Not that this was all that safe; he should really go out of the neighborhood. But he couldn't hold back, began dropping in the coins. He poked at the numbers quickly.

Harry Newman's number.

He'd found two listings for a Harry Newman, MD—his office and this one, his home. But he'd gotten nowhere trying to pinpoint the right Benjamin or B. Newman in the city or nearby suburbs. Who knew if he even lived in the state?

A woman answered, but damn if a truck wasn't going by just then; he had to wait to be heard. His back turned to the street he said, "Can you tell me where I can reach the doctor's brother? Benjamin Newman?"

"Well, he's not here. He doesn't live here."

"Could you," almost holding his breath, "tell me where he lives or give me his phone number?"

"I don't know if he'd want me to do that," she answered hesitantly. "Who is this?"

"I'm an old friend of his. I've lost track of him and been trying to reach him. I know he'd be so disappointed."

There was a pause. "Well, he is going to be here a little later. Would you like to call back? Or leave a message where he can reach you?"

After all his thinking about this, all his work, he froze. All he knew was that he mustn't just say no and hang up. "Let me make sure," he managed to say, "if I have the right Ben Newman. Is his middle name Evan?"

"I don't know, but I don't think so. In fact, I'm positive not."

He strode quickly to his car. Driving, he wanted to put his whole weight on the gas, but he mustn't get a ticket. Thinking about that made him even more nervous, which got him driving in spurts, from too fast to too slow.

There. The house.

A car was parked in the flood-lit driveway. His? He started to inch his car by, stopped for a few seconds, and then was certain he saw "MD" above the license plate.

He circled the block and parked diagonally across the street, as far from the streetlights as he could.

It was happening again, he could feel it; had started, really, when he'd sensed he was within a mile or two of the house. That he didn't feel like "Harris" anymore. It was something that always happened, slowly at first and then with a rush, each time.

He kept glancing around for a police car. They probably patrolled here pretty often, though probably never as often as back in his neighborhood, where he'd see the suckers just stop and question kids on the street.

But it wasn't as if his was the only car out here, a target for every cop. Even with all the driveways, the private garages, there were cars parked at the curbs.

He saw headlights at the far intersection, and he went a little lower in his seat. But the car didn't turn into the street. And now there were other headlights, all of them going past the corner.

And then one turned.

He dropped down deep, could see the light widening in his car, flooding it, then ebb away. Slowly he straightened up. The car had turned into Newman's driveway.

Then he saw the dark figure of a man get out and walk to the front door.

BEN AND JOANNIE carried the dishes to the kitchen, where Pat's mother was running the garbage disposal. A tall, thin woman, her face was tense, drawn. She'd barely spoken to Harry at dinner, and only just barely looked at him. And Joannie was obviously in torment.

A little later, when he and Harry were sitting alone in the living room, Harry said in a soft voice, "It was the hardest thing I ever had to do, telling them. And then the damn story never appeared."

"You did the right thing."

"But it will. It will." Harry looked away. Hands

clenched in a knot, his thumbs rubbed at each other. He'd gone to his office and the hospital today, and there'd been no reporters. But he was far from the Harry Ben had once seen in the hospital, the stethoscope curled in his pocket, walking along the hall, straight, pausing to read a nurse's chart, to nod…

Ben, looking at him, thought how his brother hadn't asked if he'd gone to the police. Probably didn't even remember him saying he would. But it didn't surprise him.

"Harry," he said, "know who I saw today? Danny Haupt."

"How is he?" But he was obviously forcing interest.

"Seems fine. He's running the hardware store. Driving through Barwyn and seeing our old house," he continued, "sure brought back a lot of memories. You know something I happened to think of? I'm sure you don't even remember this. I must have been eight, 'cause you'd just gotten your driver's license, and it was New Year's Eve and Mom and Dad were out, and I remember horns were starting to blow somewhere. You were going out driving around with Al—you two were such great buddies—and I thought I was just gonna be left behind, when you said, 'How'd you like to come with us?' That was really neat, just driving around with you guys, listening to the horns, watching people going crazy, then going to the movies and, later, I think we even stopped for hot dogs with sauerkraut."

"No," Harry said, smiling faintly, "I don't remember that."

"It was a good feeling," Ben said, "being with the big guys. I remember once—" But he didn't finish.

Harry had begun frowning slightly, was sliding the fingertips of one hand up and down the center of his chest. "What's wrong?"

"Nothing. Probably indigestion. Or I pulled something."

But his fingers gradually began rubbing harder, then his whole hand started pressing in a circle. He belched into his right fist. "It's just indigestion," he said. He rose, as Ben watched with growing alarm, then walked around slowly, occasionally nodding reassurance. He tried belching again, then sat down. His face had taken on a pallor.

"Harry."

Harry gestured that he'd be all right. But he kept rubbing the center of his chest.

"Harry." Ben stood up.

Harry started to wave him off, but then gave a quick nod. "Better get me to a hospital."

Ben hurried to him. Harry was wearing a short-sleeve shirt, and the shirt felt damp. Ben ran to the closet for a coat or jacket to pull over him. Hearing the clatter of hangers, Joannie came down, followed closely by her grandmother.

Ben said, "Look, your dad's got a little indigestion, but we're going to check it out."

Joannie's hands flew to her mouth.

Ben brought over the first thing he could grab, a raincoat. Harry winced as he put his arms through the sleeves.

Mrs. Chambers said, about to run to the phone, "I'll call nine-one-one."

"No, I'm all night," Harry protested, "I'm all right, I just want to check it out." Meanwhile he was walking with Ben to the door.

"Let me go with you!" Joannie cried.

"No, you stay here," her grandmother pleaded, her arm around her. "You stay with me."

"Joannie, I'll call as soon as I can," Ben said. "It's going to be all right."

But he was aching for her as he helped Harry into the car. He backed out of the driveway, fast. "Where the hell's a hospital?"

"Take me to Hansler." His hospital.

"Christ, that's not the closest!"

"Just—take me there. I'm all right... I'll be all right." Take that street, he said, now this, just stay on this. He kept rubbing, his face down.

Ben kept glancing over. *Don't die on me, buddy, don't do anything dumb.*

They got to the hospital soon, light-dotted in the night, and Ben made a sharp turn up the drive at the bright sign that said EMERGENCY. Braking, Ben said, "Stay put, I'll get a wheelchair, a stretcher," but Harry was already out, hunched over slightly. The doors slid open at their approach.

Ben ran ahead, got someone to bring a gurney. They rolled Harry to one of the units, Ben walking alongside, but then a nurse, starting to close the drape, motioned him out.

A woman at the desk was waiting to tap information into a computer. Her mouth made a small O when she learned that Harry was affiliated there.

Ben didn't go to the waiting room, though it was empty. He stood in the corridor where he could have a good look at that drape. For the first time he became aware of how hard he was breathing.

Though he and Harry hardly even called each other, he couldn't picture, didn't want to picture, a world without him. A world where he knew Harry wasn't there.

He found he just couldn't stand here anymore, had to walk, to move.

He went to the end of the corridor, to the waiting room, and sat on the edge of a chair where he had a clear view of the unit. After a little while he headed back there, then stopped instead and stood by the admissions desk. About ten minutes later the drape parted and a young doctor came out. Ben strode over to him.

"I'm Dr. Newman's brother, how is he?"

"Well, his EKG's normal, but his blood pressure's very high and we want to watch him overnight."

"Can I see him?"

"I don't see why not."

Harry, lying on the examination table, looked at him almost sleepily as he came in. "I'm a real pain in the ass."

Ben touched his shoulder, then squeezed it lightly, smiling. "Hey, you always were a great diagnostician."

THE EMERGENCY department doors opened to the night as Ben approached them. The tall, arched lights out there didn't really remove the blackness, only softened it.

He'd managed to calm Joannie down on the phone, even had her laughing a little about something. And her grandmother had come on and assured him that Joannie would be fine.

His car was right by the entrance, almost blocking it. It was only when he drove out to the street that he realized he'd forgotten to turn on his headlights.

He was suddenly confused, didn't know how the hell to get back to the apartment.

He decided to just go straight, and after awhile a street became familiar, and then he knew where he was going. He pulled into his building's parking lot, turned off the lights, got out and locked the doors.

The lot was a hazy mixture of night and light. He walked through the grayness, past lines of cars, and then into the bright lights of the lobby.

IT HAD BEEN frustrating enough losing Ben Newman in traffic, but to come back to the brother's house and wait for hours and not have either of them show up!

It wasn't midnight yet, it wasn't even eleven-thirty, yet one by one the lights in the house, and now the one on the driveway, were going out.

And all he had of Ben Newman was just the first three numbers of his license plate.

THIRTEEN

BEN, WAKING TO darkness, thought it was still night, but when he got out of bed and opened the drapes, sunlight burst in. A quick look at his watch told him it was after ten. He hated sleeping late though he'd obviously needed it.

Suddenly anxious, he called the hospital—he hadn't had a thought of Harry until now. He learned that Harry had been moved out of coronary care, but was sedated and wasn't to receive calls for a while. He quickly called Joannie. They'd learned the same thing.

Later, over a cup of coffee, he wondered what to do this morning. He'd see Harry later, and he wasn't up to working. He thought of the art museum, then maybe going over to the Rodin, a little museum a short distance down the Parkway from it. Maybe, but Saturday with its crowds wasn't his favorite day for museums.

He wondered about calling a friend. But there was no one he really felt like seeing, and there wasn't an important woman in his life since he and Corinne broke up last month. Although they'd had great times together he wasn't sorry. She would be all wrong for someone who lived the freelance life.

He had told Nancy Dean he would call her after he saw Dan; but though he would like to see her again, he found himself resisting it. It just seemed off-the-wall after all these years and, for some reason, who she was. He couldn't even hold onto a single image of her. She kept changing back and forth from the Nancy sitting across the restaurant booth from him, right out of *Vogue,* to the girl in grammar school who was the first he remembered there wearing long earrings, to the girl with the tightest-ass jeans hanging out in that luncheonette a few blocks from the high school.

He called. Her voice answered against the background of a copying machine popping out paper. "Oh, hi," she said, "hold on a second." She turned off the machine, then said again, "Hi."

"It sounds like the Ford plant," he said. "You didn't tell me you owned *that.*"

"Not quite," she laughed. "In fact, I'm the only one here. Everyone's sick."

"Could you use a two-finger typist?"

"I could even use an elbow typist."

He laughed. "For elbows I charge big. But look, seriously, you need help?"

"No, really. Thanks. I'm mostly doing copying."

"I know you're busy, I won't hold you. But I wanted you to know it was great seeing you again."

"It was awfully nice seeing you. I enjoyed it."

"And I wanted to tell you what I've been doing. I saw Dan but it added up to nothing." He told her something of their conversation, then about going to see Nevon, and then about the visit from Ed Gowan. "He really didn't tell me anything I didn't know," he said. He waited for her to say something, then when she didn't: "Do you see him around much? He told me he still lives in Barwyn."

"Not in a long time. But once in a while I see his wife."

"I used to hate his guts. But he seems all right." He was looking toward the window, at the sunlight, at the clear sky above the center city buildings. "Hey, can I be the devil? Can I tempt you away from your work today?"

"Oh...I really can't, I'm sorry."

"It's such a beautiful day. I thought maybe a ride somewhere."

"No, I'm afraid not. I'm sorry."

"I'm one hell of a lousy devil." He felt, surprisingly, a deep sense of disappointment.

"I—" She stopped, then after a long pause, "Look. It's now what? I don't even have my watch."

"It's almost ten-thirty."

"Could you give me a couple hours?"

JULIA NEUBAUER, a short, slightly-built woman of thirty-one, set down her luggage, took her house key from her shoulder bag and opened the door. Susann, behind her, carried in Julia's carry-all by the hook and put it on the sofa. She said, "Should I take it upstairs?"

"No, that's fine. You know, I'm so damn mad at myself. I set the automatics all wrong." She began going around switching off lights on the first floor of her brick rowhouse in the Mount Airy section of Philadelphia. "I had the lights on in the day and off at night. I'm so dumb. I'm lucky this place is in one piece."

Susann, who was four years older and considerably taller, came over and took her hand. She smiled.

"You're always mad at yourself for something. Forget it. Didn't we have a great time?"

"God, yes." Julia smiled and squeezed her hand. They had been in Key West for two weeks—there'd been such a feeling of freedom there. "I just don't want it to be over."

Susann held Julia to her tightly. "When do you think you're going to do it?"

"Like I told you. Monday. I'm going to the realtor's Monday."

Susann drew back her head and smiled. Then she brought her close again and kissed her lightly on the lips. "I'll talk to you later," she whispered, though she didn't have to whisper.

Julia nodded quickly. She stood in the doorway until Susann got in her car. Susann waved at her from behind the wheel, then drove off as Julia waved back.

Julia closed the door, double-locking it. She took a deep breath.

It felt a little eerie coming home to this house, the house where she'd lived with her grandmother until her death, just three weeks ago. Still, if it wasn't for the neighborhood she'd have Susann sell her place and move in here instead of the other way around. But the kids around here, they'd probably stone the place.

She reflected on Key West—the girls they'd met, even the guys were nice. It had been the first time she had let go. Susann had been so understanding these past couple of months since they'd met.

She started to take one of the bags upstairs, then remembered and went to the answering machine in the kitchen. She pressed a button and the tape rewound itself, then went forward. The first call was from a stock broker she'd never heard of. Then, one by one, nine in all: Hang up, buzz, hang up, buzz.

EACH TIME Ben drove through Barwyn he saw something that came as surprisingly new to him. This time it was Spitz's, though it had an Asian name now, where they used to buy candy and comic books and, for a while until some parents learned about it and there was all that fuss, they were able to buy chances on boxes of candy.

He was passing the main path into the woods that used to be the jungle of Africa to Danny and him, with their lunches from home and, sometimes, a few cigarettes Danny would snag for them to smoke sitting back against a tree. Ahead now was Barwyn Elementary, and after that would be the turn to her house.

He pulled to the curb instead.

He felt strange about this, about being so deliberate. About stopping at a drugstore first.

"WHERE," BEN ASKED in the car, "would you like to go?"

"Anywhere," she said, "as long as it's out of the city."

"Let's see." He looked at her, trying to think of places. She looked so damn pretty; it was the only word for it. She'd had on big round sunglasses when they had come out of her house, but she'd put them on the dashboard and her eyes looked even greener than before. She was wearing a light blue pullover, with a white collar showing, and a patterned, summery skirt. Her jagged red hair glistened, almost as if wet.

"How about New Hope?" he suggested. "Have you been there recently?"

"No, that sounds wonderful. I haven't been there for at least three years. And the last time wasn't really New Hope, but up that way. It was on a pollution thing."

He looked over at her curiously. "You do pollution?"

"Well, I belonged to a group that took on environmental issues. Picketing, things like that. And we went up to help out in Bucks County. The usual story—a plant pouring its guts out. We had a bit of a problem with the police."

"You went to jail?"

"Just for a night."

"Just for a night? You couldn't make it for more?" She laughed, and he said, "I'm impressed." And it wasn't something he was simply saying.

"Don't be. There were an awful lot of us. I felt sorry for the police having to carry me to the van, so I walked. And we weren't supposed to."

"Without getting too personal, do you spend much time in stir?"

She smiled. "No, that was my first and only. And it was very scary. Actually, though, I tried to get arrested two times before that, but they wouldn't take me."

"Now *that's* rejection."

"It sounds funny but it's true. They took just about everyone but me. This one time we were all chained to the same fence."

"You chain, too? God, I got a winner."

She smiled again. Then she settled her head back and stared ahead. "It is a beautiful day," she said.

"Isn't it? I'm glad you could come."

"It's just that I'm so damn compulsive. When I have something to do I have to do it yesterday."

They'd been driving for a while on I-95, with the Delaware River on their right, in view between factories. But now the highway was curving past large, single homes, then an occasional farmhouse and grassland, and once, somehow out of place, what looked like an industrial park. She was staring out her window.

"Do you want the radio on?" he asked.

"No." She looked at him with a faint smile, then out her window again. It was a silence she obviously enjoyed, didn't want to break.

About a half hour out of the city he turned off the highway and they drove for another fifteen minutes along a tree-edged canal, past stone farmhouse-looking homes and Revolutionary War sites, and finally onto a street that led into the village of New Hope.

"I'm glad you thought of this," she said.

"This is one of the times of the year I love best. Spring and Fall. In fact, the last time I was here was in the Fall. The leaves were absolutely magnificent, and we ate someplace with a big log fire. I even remember what I had—duck. I'll never forget that duck...only," he corrected himself, "I didn't have duck. Pheasant."

"And wild rice?"

"How did you know? Hey, was I with you?"

"Don't you remember the dress?"

They both laughed. She put on her sunglasses.

The village, usually packed with tourists, wasn't particularly crowded for a warm Saturday in April. He found a parking spot easily on one of the streets, and put in a couple of hours' worth of quarters.

They walked along streets filled with crafts shops, antique shops, boutiques, little restaurants. None of the shopkeepers seemed to care if anyone bought or not: they kept reading their newspaper or playing with their cat or staring out the front window; would turn or look up only to answer a question, or smile when you said goodbye.

At an antique shop, Nancy saw a scraggly fur belt of leopard skin and she made an expression of nausea. Some small earrings caught her attention but, no, she didn't really want them.

They walked on, in the clear bright air. Over there was the Bucks County Playhouse, and there the canal again, with some bobbing ducks to one side. A mule-drawn barge was carrying people along it. Now there were clopping sounds behind them, and a horse and carriage passed them on the street, a flaxen-haired driver in high hat holding the reins, and a young couple and child looking around.

Ben said, "What do you feel like eating?"

"Nothing very much, really. Just a sandwich."

They went to a place overlooking the canal. They both settled on the same thing, simultaneously— shrimp salad sandwiches, on pumpernickel. They laughed at that, but then when she ordered iced tea, he ordered coffee.

"And here," he said, "I thought we had everything in common."

They got back to the car almost two hours after the meter ran out, but there wasn't a ticket.

"Are you always this lucky?" she asked.

"No, you must be. I was going to make you pay for it."

She laughed and lifted her glasses onto her hair and waited until he unlocked the doors.

Driving back she said, "You know, I was just thinking of something. I remember being in—I think it was the fourth grade with you."

"Really?" He didn't know why he should be surprised. After all, he remembered her.

"And you know what I used to think? I remember thinking, what must it be like to be smart?"

"Yeah? I've often wondered that myself."

"I was so dumb. I don't know if I was really dumb, but I felt so dumb."

"That's terrible."

He had the feeling of wanting to stop the car, to just sit and look at her. No, he really wanted to hold her.

"The only time I didn't feel dumb was when—when I was with kids I thought were dumb. But I guess I made them feel smart, too. But you—all of the Ellen-types—you were all from a different world."

He kept glancing over at her. Then, staring ahead, "It's so damn strange. I used to think I was pretty much the only stranger there. I thought I was just about the only one from a different world." She was looking at him, frowning. "It seemed," he said, "like everyone's family lived in Barwyn a hundred years."

"Mine didn't."

"I thought just about everyone's did." He wouldn't have thought he'd ever be telling her this, but suddenly it was easy. "Everyone else's parents seemed to have been born in this country, even the Jews there."

As he pulled up in front of her house, she put her sunglasses in her shoulder bag and took out her key. She looked over at him and smiled.

"I had a wonderful time."

"I'm glad. So did I."

He took her hand. It was surprisingly cold. So was the other one. "Hey," he said. He took the left one between his hands and rubbed it; then the other. "You know, I've been known to burst people into flames."

She smiled. He could feel her fingers squeeze his; then they went limp. He leaned over and lifted her chin with his finger, looked at her eyes, then kissed her on the lips. Her hands were on his arms; then she drew back, breathing hard.

"I'm going to say goodnight," she said.

He started to open his door, to go around to hers, but she took his arm again. Though she was still breathing hard she shook her head when he tried to kiss her. He touched her cheek; she put her hand over his, lightly, then turned slightly and kissed it.

She looked at him. "Goodnight."

"Goodnight, Nan."

He watched her go.

FOURTEEN

THE LAST THING Julia Neubauer felt like doing that day she'd come back from Key West was going food shopping. But she had come home to nothing in the refrigerator. She was holding off as long as she could, with other tasks, putting away things from the trip, making a few calls, then going into the basement with a large load of wash.

She had just turned the machine on when she heard the phone. She hurried upstairs, sure it was Susann even though she had called earlier.

She swept it up from its cradle on the wall. "Hello? Hello?" she said into the silent phone.

STARING AHEAD at her house from the car, he was having trouble again staying "Harris." Each solid thump of his heart seemed to be trying to drive him from his name.

But he must hold onto it—he was Harris, would always be Harris.

He wasn't even sure if she was the same Julia Neubauer. But even if she was, he didn't have a plan.

Which was why he deliberately hadn't brought anything along, not his knife and certainly not his gun. He didn't want to be tempted, as he knew he could easily be, into doing something reckless.

The house—he just wanted to take a look at the house.

It was the worst kind, a row. Neighbors like skin on each side. And a wall of neighbors facing it across the street, and another wall behind it across a driveway. Almost every house had a car at the curb.

Lights were on downstairs in her house; upstairs was dark.

He didn't know if she lived alone or with a dozen people.

The only thing he could think to do was keep waiting here, even until morning if he had to, to see who came out. Then once he knew, he could make it look like anything. Maybe a break-in, perhaps like she'd come home to a burglar who used one of her kitchen knives. Or it could be a fatal mugging somewhere.

Frowning, he leaned forward slightly, thinking he'd seen a sliver of light in the doorway. It was gone now, but he was suddenly sure he'd seen it, that someone must have opened the door a little, then closed it. Grimacing, he kept his eyes on the door, trying to will it open.

There.

The light burst on, a woman stepped through the front door, then turned to face it as she closed it. He could see her, just a dark figure walking quickly down the steps to the sidewalk. She surely went to her car, but he couldn't see it since he was parked behind several cars on her side of the street. Then he heard the sound of a motor, then saw light spread along the street as the car pulled out.

He started the motor, but waited until she was near the corner before starting to follow. He followed her across the intersection, then through a couple of turns and finally, lingering a distance behind, onto the mostly-empty parking lot of a supermarket. He waited until she was walking into the store before he parked.

He could see her through the store window, but only her back. She was behind a line of shopping carts, tugging one free.

As the door inside the market slid open in front of her, he saw part of her jacket and tan skirt disappearing into an aisle. He started to walk after her, to try to get close enough to see her face, but the vast emptiness of the place stopped him. He'd not only be conspicuous to her but a clerk might remember him later.

He pretended to look at some free pamphlets on a rack, his back to the checkout counters, then walked out.

He parked close to the entrance.

After about twenty minutes she came out with a filled cart. And there under the lights, as if suddenly trying to remember something, she looked toward the sky, a hand over her mouth.

And now as the hand slowly came down, the face revealed enough of itself to become once again that little face, so smug, so *ugly,* so pleased above her extended arms as she'd showed her shit from aisle to aisle.

He kept staring at her as she pushed the cart to her car.

If only it wasn't so brightly lighted here!

But where else?

He watched as she opened the trunk, as she started to put the bags away.

He kept watching her, then started the car, afraid of what he might do. He drove off, trying to calm himself, urging himself to use his brains. He headed back to her street but a car was parked in his old spot; the only spot open was right in front of her house.

He didn't want that; he wanted to leave it empty for her.

He circled the block and double-parked a few houses away and turned off the motor, the lights.

Soon a car turned the corner behind him, went by him, now was backing in there.

He looked at her as she came out and opened the trunk. She set several bags on the ground, then closed the door and began lifting them up. Then she lowered them again, though he didn't know why.

Until he saw her looking out at the street, then down at one of the bags that lay on its side, its contents spilled out.

She went out to the street, began picking things up.

With her left hand! He'd forgotten she was left-handed!

And in that instant he turned on the motor, and almost stood on the gas pedal.

FIFTEEN

MANY OF THE PEOPLE Catherine Cassaway would see in church had been pupils of hers. Including the minister. And this Sunday was the first in so long that one of them, poor, tragic Ellen, hadn't been there with her husband and daughter.

It had certainly cast a shadow.

Miss Cassaway was in line as usual after services to shake hands with and say a few words to the minister, who was standing inside the doorway of the Methodist church. From here she could see that it had become windy—women were holding their hats to their heads as they walked down the steps to the sidewalk.

"I enjoyed it as usual," she told him, and the minister took her hand and said with a smile, "Thank you. I hope you feel as well as you look."

"I'm doing just fine," she said.

He pressed her hand before releasing it and now she too was holding onto her hat, a little turquoise circle with a short veil that covered her brow. Though he'd been here about fourteen years, it was still hard to think of him as her pastor. He had been one of those fairly good students—far from excellent but fairly good—who could be mischievous at times, though not bad. There was a big difference but she had always found, and still did today, that you mustn't go easier on one than the other.

A hand took her arm as her raincoat blew open when she was halfway down the steps. She turned quickly, annoyed: she hated being *grabbed*. Even being physically helped.

It was Mrs. Tilman, the wife of another former pupil.

"No, no, I'm doing just fine," Catherine Cassaway said firmly, taking her arm back and pulling her coat together.

Mrs. Tilman, her face red, said with an embarrassed little laugh, "I know you are. I was trying to hold onto you."

Miss Cassaway, still clutching her coat, entered the crowd on the sidewalk, buttoning the coat as she walked.

Hello, Miss Cassaway, or nods here and there, a smile. Every Sunday it was like this. She walked with the wind to the corner—it was pushing her as she passed the crowd—where she stood in a short line to buy a *Dispatch* from a boy at a makeshift stand. In her car she dropped the heavy paper next to her. Her heart was beating fast. She'd been terrified as she'd made her way down those steps in the wind and as she'd walked, fighting its push, to the car. She couldn't help but think of what she'd heard about Ellen's accident. If a young person like that could lose her balance or trip on such familiar steps, how much easier for an older person to fall or make a misstep! And then what they'd say about you—feeble, even senile!

Now, her thoughts drifting to something else as she began driving home, she couldn't help but feel a touch of bitterness. And she promised herself firmly to give up that stupid hope—that someone one day would sidle up to her or call her and say, "Look, I'm not supposed to tell you…" That there'd be something special for her at the bicentennial, not just being honored with all the other "long-timers." After all, forty-two years, the longest of *any* of the elementary school teachers in Barwyn.

No more of that. She didn't need that.

Parked in front of her house, she took hold of the newspaper and after locking the car fought the wind as she went up the path. Then all at once she stopped and shook her head in disgust. It had happened again! A few pages of a newspaper were scattered around, most of them flattened against her bushes.

And here she'd *called* the *Dispatch* and had *told* them they were delivering the papers to her by mistake.

Angry—it was enough that she saw this kind of carelessness and incompetence in school all day, and now more than ever out in the world—she started to bend over to gather up some of the pages. But then she noticed that the bulk of the paper lay on her next-door neighbor's lawn, some of its pages flapping, and realized that it hadn't been delivered to her but had blown into her yard from over there.

THAT SUNDAY MORNING, finding that he'd run out of coffee, Ben went down to the lobby to have breakfast in the apartment's public coffee shop. Afterward he would go see Harry. They were keeping him in the hospital at least one more day.

He'd already skimmed through the news sections of the *Dispatch* up in his apartment, in a rush to see if there was anything about Harry. But good, no. Now he could read it leisurely, though always looking for stories he could use, of crimes or something that might trigger an idea for an article or book. He found two possibilities, both of them murders, one in the Poconos, the other over in New Jersey. He tore them out as carefully as he could, but the sound of the ripping lifted the curiosity and heads of a middle-aged couple in the booth across from him.

His eyes soon focused on a large picture on the third page. He went to it quickly because of the kind of picture it was, and the headline. A picture of a woman in an almost fetal position on the street, an ambulance in the background, a paramedic bent over her. And the headline: HIT-AND-RUN VICTIM.

But after reading the caption and not recognizing the name, he turned the page.

"HARRIS"—FOR YEARS just about everyone called him by his last name—"will you come here?"

For a moment he sat as though impaled. Today more than ever it came like a knife, hearing his name called without warning. And there was anger in the boss's voice.

He got up from the set he'd been working on and went over to the end of the bench where his boss was examining a set.

"You look at this? You see this?"

He saw it instantly: he'd neglected to weld one of the connections. He started to reach for a soldering iron but his hand began shaking.

"Hey." His boss grabbed his arm. "What the devil's wrong with you?"

"I'm"—trying to think—"I got a little flu, I think."

"Flu?" His boss pulled back from him. "Look, I don't need any flu, don't breathe on me. Gimme." He took back the soldering iron.

Back at his stool, he found that his hands were shaking even more, that his boss and Vince, the only other worker in the place, were occasionally glancing over at him. But he managed to get the set done, put it on a shelf behind him, and carried another one over to the bench. But as he was putting it down it landed with a thump—his fingers had given out.

"Harris," his boss said, his voice patient but strained, "go home. Take care of yourself."

"I'm okay."

"Go to bed, do whatever you have to, I need you tomorrow. We got a big day tomorrow."

He looked at his boss, then stood up and put on his windbreaker that lay on the next stool.

"Take care of yourself," Vince said.

"I'll see you." Had to say something, try to act normal. It was the only reason he'd agreed to come in on a Sunday when his boss called this morning.

He walked out into the wind, hands in the pockets of his windbreaker, then stopped at the corner and peered around to take a look at his car, a little up the block. He'd deliberately parked there, away from the store in case someone had spotted it last night. He tried to see if anyone might be watching it. As far as he could tell, no. But that didn't mean the police weren't around, in an unmarked car or even in one of those houses, just waiting for someone to show up.

The hand in his right pocket lay over a .38 special snubnose.

It was only the second or third time since coming to the city that he carried it with him. But last night was the first time he'd lost his head like that and might have gone for it if he'd had it on him.

He began walking to the car, his arms, his legs almost rigid.

He'd spent half the night getting all her blood he could see off the car. And was lucky he hadn't smashed a headlight or grille. Lucky too it was such an old bugger of a car, dented, part of the front bumper even pulled away; so dented no one would notice new ones.

Still, even with the headlights turned off, someone might have gotten his license.

He opened the door and slid in quickly. The car started immediately. As he drove, his eyes kept shifting from the side mirror to the rearview. No one seemed to be following. But why would they follow, wouldn't they have just grabbed him there?

If anything, they might be waiting at home.

There too he parked around the corner; walked slowly, head straight, but glancing to each side.

In his apartment, he almost went limp against the locked door. He sank on a chair and held his face.

After all his being careful, being careful, how could he have done that, how could he have just let go? But it was as though something had burst in his brain.

He took off his windbreaker and put the gun on the kitchen table.

If they came after him he had enough rounds to kill half an army and then himself. It wasn't dying that scared him; that didn't scare him at all—it was dying before he was finished.

Afterward, well, afterward, he wouldn't care.

He opened a cabinet drawer and took out a black-and-white composition book he'd bought a few months ago but still had trouble using. Each time he sat down with it, something in him rebelled; he was terrible at writing, always had to be so careful. He took the book and a ballpoint pen over to the kitchen table. He glanced briefly at the last things he'd written, then turned to a fresh page. He stared at it a long while before starting to write.

But he didn't do more than a couple of lines when he saw that some words were just a scribble. He crossed them out, started to go on, then stopped.

He looked at the page, then carefully ripped it out, making sure to pull out the loose, connecting page at the back.

This time he printed slowly in block letters.

MY NAME IS CHARLES HARRIS. I WANT IT ON MY GRAVE.

A NURSE WAS coming out of Harry's room as Ben approached it. The room was bright, nicely appointed—apparently a VIP room. Harry was sitting in a chair in his robe.

Harry smiled vaguely at him; he looked half-asleep. "Hi."

It was good, a little surprising, to see the smile. "How you doing, buddy?" Ben put his hand on his arm.

"Great." But he immediately looked away, and tears filmed his eyes. "Christ," he said when he looked back, "I have a hard time getting this goddamn hospital to keep my patients, *heart* patients, three days, but they don't want to get rid of me. They must love me."

"Maybe they do."

"They think I'm crazy, that's what they think."

"They think you're exhausted, that's what they think."

"I'm so loaded with shit, they've got me so loaded." He rubbed at his forehead, closing his eyes. "Go home," he said without looking up.

"I just got here, buddy."

He shrugged without opening his eyes. "Go home."

Ben watched him as he was sinking into sleep. But then Harry's head bobbed and his eyes snapped open. But he didn't seem to be aware that Ben was there; he just stared. Ben glanced at his watch, then back at him. He wanted to call Nancy, couldn't wait to call her, but he didn't want to leave while Harry was awake. He watched Harry as his eyes slowly began to close again. And then stayed closed.

He stood up quietly and went out to the hall. He called Nancy from a pay phone outside the visitors' lounge, explained he was at the hospital but would be leaving in an hour at the most and was wondering if she was up to seeing him again.

"Oh..." She sounded genuinely pained. "A friend's over and I have to go somewhere with her." She paused. "But I'll be home about seven. If you're not too fussy, would you like dinner?"

"CAN I HELP?" Ben asked from the entrance to the kitchen.

"Yes," she said, without turning from the stove, "by staying where you are and talking to me."

"Let's see. Do you think this is a good time to buy wheat futures?"

She looked at him over her shoulder and smiled. She turned back to the stove, where she was stir-frying chopped chicken breasts, potatoes and peppers. It was sizzling on the burner.

"It could use ginger," she said, shaking the pan slightly, "but I don't have any. I thought I did. Lucky I have garlic."

"You never told me you didn't have ginger," he said sternly.

She looked at him again and smiled, then opened the oven to see if the rolls were warm enough. She had on brown slacks and loafers, the sleeves of her peach blouse pushed up at the elbows.

She'd already set the table, on the other side of the divider in the large kitchen. There was a centerpiece of mums on the bright-white tablecloth. She brought over the pan and portioned it out while he got the rolls. As soon as she sat down she started to jump up. "I forgot to make salad."

"Whoa. Whoa." He touched her arm. "If you need it, fine. I don't. Really."

"You sure?"

"I lie about everything but salad."

She smiled and sank back. You couldn't buy wine in the state on Sunday, and he'd found himself out of it in his liquor cabinet, but she had a little chianti left in an old, straw-bound bottle. He divided it, then held out his glass to hers.

"All I want to wish for you," he said, "is merely the best."

"And you. And I hope your brother feels better real soon."

He nodded appreciatively. "Delicious," he said after the first bite. Then, as she was about to say something quickly, he said, "Yes. I know. It could use ginger."

"I was going to say I'm glad it doesn't have ginger."

They laughed together, then she wanted to know did he like to cook.

"Do I cook? Someday I'll make you my chili. But be warned, it's been known to turn on fire alarms."

"Oh my, and here I was going to make chili."

"In other words, you don't make it real hot."

"No," she said defiantly, "I don't mean that at all. You have to be at least eighteen to eat my chili."

He laughed. "Why do people who ordinarily get along very well, argue about their chili?"

"Do they?"

"I don't know. It sounded good."

She laughed with him. Later as she was pouring coffee, she said quietly, frowning, "I just remembered. Did you see the story in this morning's paper about a woman who was hit in a hit-and-run?"

"I saw the picture but I didn't read it. I just glanced at it. Why?"

"Did you happen to see her name?"

"I did, though I've forgotten it. Why?"

"Julia Neubauer? It's a name I think I know, but I can't remember. I think someone by that name lived around here years ago."

Ben thought. No, he still couldn't place it.

"Well," she said. "Anyway."

She finished pouring the coffee.

He sat on the sofa, she on a chair angled toward it, sharing a coffee table.

"This room," she said, "was originally the dining room, but when I made the living room into the office, I converted this into the living room."

"Would you run that by me again?" he said.

"When there's more than two living rooms in a sentence I get confused."

"This," she said very slowly, "was originally the dining room, and that—"

"Was a bedroom," he said.

She looked at him, glowering. He smiled. "I'm sorry. I feel good. And I don't know how to handle it."

She smiled. "I'm glad." Setting down her cup, she asked, "When do you think your brother will be coming home?"

"They say maybe tomorrow."

"Oh, that's good."

"But I don't know, I'm not sure." He hadn't told her anything about Harry being under suspicion, had no idea if she'd seen the picture of the two of them leaving police headquarters. Although he wanted to protect Harry, shield him, somehow it had become important that he be open with her. "I don't know if you know anything about what's been happening with him," he said.

She listened solemnly as he told her.

"I know Harry," he said. "There's no way he could have—" He shook his head. "No way. But I've probably been acting like a nut, trying to tie it up with the damn bicentennial."

"I don't see where that's acting like a nut."

He looked at her. He wanted to tell her more, but he wasn't even sure of it in his own mind—how it seemed as if all his life half of him was angry at Harry, the other half wanting to put his arms around him, and how it was that way now.

He kept looking at her. Then he reached out his hand. At first she just looked at him. Then her hand came out, and he took it. He rubbed her fingers, the palm, the back. She came into his arms and they kissed, then she put her head against his shoulder.

He was aware, holding her, how all evening he still couldn't keep her fixed in his head. How she kept changing from the kid with the long earrings and the guys sucking on cigarettes around her, to this woman with the big eyes and the very gentle look. He wasn't sure if he even had her fixed now; but almost. He found himself wanting to feel her skin to the very pores; feel through her hair to her scalp.

His hands moved along her back, gentle at first, then hard. He started to lift her chin but stopped when he felt slight resistance.

He let her settle back.

"Just this," she said softly, her head turned on his shoulder. "Please. Just this."

SIXTEEN

THE NEXT MORNING'S *Dispatch* ran an item about
Harry in its most widely read gossip column.

THE NEXT MORNING'S *Dispatch* ran an item about
Harry in its most widely read gossip column.

> We hear that cardiologist Harry Newman, whose
> wife Patricia was found dead under mysterious
> circumstances in the swimming pool of their
> Chestnut Hill home, has been admitted to Hansler
> Hospital for undisclosed reasons. The only visi-
> tors he's permitted are family members. Dr. New-
> man is, incidentally, a member of the Hansler
> staff.

Ben lowered the paper slowly. The goddamn thing
did everything but name Harry as a suspect. He wondered who planted it. It could be someone at Hansler
who didn't like him. But he'd bet anything it was the
police, nipping at him, trying to pressure and break
him from a distance.

NANCY WAS ON the phone a few minutes later.

"You all right?" she asked, and he sensed without
her telling him that she'd seen the item.

"I'm okay. I'm fine."

"Do you remember," she said, after a pause, "my
saying thought I knew Julia Neubauer? The victim in

the hit-and-run? Well, a friend just called to ask if I
saw in the paper this morning that she died, and to
ask if I remembered her from church and way back in
grammar school. My friend reminded me who she
was. You might remember her—she was in your
class.''

Ben frowned, trying to place the name, to put it with
a face. But he couldn't. ''Who told you this?'

''Do you remember Charleen DePolitto from your
class? Tall, long black hair?''

''I sort of remember the name.''

''Anyway, she called. And it really hit me, what
with what's been happening.''

Four now? ''Nan, I've got the paper here but I
haven't read it carefully yet. Tell me, I don't remember, where did this happen?''

''Right in front of her house. She went food shopping and apparently dropped a bag while unloading
her car and then she was hit when she tried to pick
the stuff up off the street. It's just that it's such a
coincidence,'' she said.

''Do you know if she was connected with the bicentennial?''

''I know she wasn't on any of the committees.''

But George Havers, he was thinking, hadn't been
either. ''Nan, would you be able to find out if she was
involved with it in any way? It could be anything—
an award, maybe being in the parade. I don't know.
Anything.''

''I'll try. I'll make some calls.''

THE STORY, along with her picture, was on the obituary page. He looked at the thin, youngish face, but

couldn't place it. But her age, thirty-one, would be right. She'd returned from a two-week vacation in Key West the same day she'd been hit. She was a graduate of the University of Pennsylvania, had been a social worker, did charity work for her church. Quotes from friends and colleagues centered on her warmth and kindness. Only an aunt and uncle were mentioned as relatives.

He looked at her picture again.

A serious face, almost grim, with no trace of a smile. He couldn't picture makeup on it, but he could her hair in curlers.

What could she possibly have to do with his sister-in-law, with Ellen and George?

He picked up the phone. No, Information told him, there was no listing for a Julia Neubauer. And no, none for a J. Neubauer either.

A few minutes later he was driving to the main library, on the Parkway. He sat down with three weeks' editions of the *Dispatch*.

He began going through them slowly, column by column, even the smallest ads and letters to the editor. But this week's papers, nothing. Last week's, nothing either—no, he'd just skimmed one page and so went back to it—but no, nothing. He started the third week's. Nothing. Nothing.

And then the name grabbed him.

JULIA NEUBAUER

Startled, he couldn't take his eyes from it for a moment.

DIED: CHILDREN'S AUTHOR

Julia Neubauer, 84, whose stories charmed children decades ago, died in her home last night. Mrs. Neubauer, who was widowed this year...

The obituary went on to give the titles of her five books, the last of which was published in the 1970s. She had been active in church work and...

the anti-vivisection movement. Mrs. Neubauer, who lived with her granddaughter, Julia...

Fingers suddenly tight on the page, he looked quickly at the date. Less than a week before Julia left on the trip. And Julia had been killed the same night she'd returned.

He strode to one of the public phones.

"Nancy, I'm sorry if I'm interrupting something, but I couldn't wait to tell you."

Afterward she said simply, "My God," and then nothing for a few moments. "But, Ben, I don't see where it could have anything to do with the bicentennial. I've made a few calls. Unless it's some damn fluke, she wasn't in it, had nothing to do with it. They'd know. I talked to Charleen DePolitto again. I wanted to see if she knew anything more about her. I thought Julia'd gone to Barwyn High a couple of years, but Charleen said no. She went to Girls High."

Back at the table, he started to lift the pile of papers to return them to the desk, then sat back again.

Pat. Ellen. George. Julia. He couldn't think of anything that linked the four of them.

Not the bicentennial anymore, that was out. And not Barwyn High—Julia hadn't gone there. And not Barwyn Elementary, since his sister-in-law had gone to Madsen Elementary.

He frowned, then the frown gradually turned into a look of astonishment. Barwyn Elementary. They'd all gone there—except for Pat.

Pat the mistake.

SEVENTEEN

DRIVING BACK to the apartment he debated with himself whether to take this to Detective McGlynn.

Bill, these murders may have nothing to do with the bicentennial after all.

Yeah. He could just hear the sarcasm, maybe outright anger, that here he was with still another theory.

And who the hell could blame him? Why would anyone kill three adults who had not only attended the same grammar school but had been in the same class? Grammar school! One of the kids? A teacher gone berserk over an old, old grudge?

Soon, though, another name flashed through his mind. Ed Gowan. He still didn't like the guy and talking to him would probably be a waste of time, but after all he did know Barwyn, knew the people, perhaps the feuds, the affairs, whatever. Maybe, just maybe, crimes that had their roots back then, back *in childhood* in that tight community, would make some kind of sense to him.

But when Ben called him, Gowan, after listening to what he had to say, said, "Let me ask you something. Your name happened to come up. You write for those detective magazines, don't you?"

"That's right."

"So you're the guy who helped that guy get out of the can."

Ben didn't answer right away, aware that Gowan hadn't been able to bring himself to even say Jerry Tomavich's name. "I did some work on it."

"Hell, you did a great job. Great. But what I'm saying is this. It could happen, couldn't it, that by some fluke, some miracle, I could write a half-decent story or even a book? I mean, say, about something that's right down my alley?"

"Yeah," Ben said, knowing where he was going. "It might even be a terrific one."

"But that doesn't mean that me, an amateur, could get lucky and do another good one, does it? Well, being a cop's like that. Don't take offense, but you did good once and that could have put some ideas in your head about what it takes. But that was that and this is this. So. I'm sorry, but no matter what you say, Ellen's death was an accident. And that kills your theory. It's as simple as that."

IT'S AS SIMPLE as that.

The words had become claws in his brain.

Still, he managed to write a few pages of a story before pushing himself away from the computer. Something else was beginning to compete for his thoughts. His old elementary-school graduation picture.

His mother had had it, and he had no idea what happened to it. He remembered that it had been taken in the schoolyard, against the front of the building, the smaller kids sitting in front on a long bench, the others standing in rows behind them.

He tried recalling the faces, hoping that one would

emerge that with some great straining of memory and imagination could conceivably tie in with the deaths. But offhand he couldn't think of more than eight kids out of the whole class, three of them George and Ellen and Danny. And all of whom he remembered as great kids.

He wondered where he could get hold of a picture, thought first of Dan Haupt. But he'd as soon not go to him. Then he remembered Nancy's friend, Charleen DePolitto.

"Yes, I'll call her," Nancy told him. "I'll call you back as soon as I hear."

When the phone rang a few minutes later he thought it was her. But it was Harry.

"Want you to know," Harry said in a heavy voice, "I'm still here. But don't want you to bother coming."

"How do you feel?"

"Great." But it was thick with sarcasm. "Just great."

"Did you talk to the doctor today?"

"What the hell does he know? I'm really calling to say I'm getting the hell out of here."

"Wait a second, wait. Tell me, why do they say they want to keep you?"

"I had an extra heartbeat last night but I checked out all right this morning. Still, they want to watch me. It's all bullshit, I've had this before, I know what it is, it's just nerves, it's just everything." After a moment he added, "I saw that fuckin' thing in the paper."

"Harry, you've got to blow it off. You can't let that get to you."

"It's not getting to me, it's not getting to me! I'm

just saying." Then he said, "I'm here, everyone thinks I'm guilty."

"Then it is that."

"Don't try to analyze me!"

Here again was the quick temper Ben knew from the time he was a kid. His own started to rise but he put it down. "Harry," he cautioned, "this is a public phone, remember."

"I don't give a damn. I know what I'm guilty of and it's not that. I want to get out of here."

"Tell me about the irregular heartbeat."

"I've told you, it's nothing, it's gone!"

"Did you tell them you want to go home?"

Harry didn't answer right away. Then he said, "No, what's the difference?" And something about the way he said it made Ben think he was actually afraid to leave, afraid of his health maybe, or maybe his sanity. Or maybe of what was out there waiting.

HE PICKED Nancy up early that evening to drive to Charleen DePolitto's. She did have a class picture.

"This is Line Number One," he said as they pulled away, "but you look especially pretty tonight."

"Really?" She looked over at him, smiling.

"Well, maybe I need another look. I can't tell at this distance."

She slid closer. They looked at each other. Her lips, open in a smile, closed as he kissed her quickly.

"Really," he said. It was true. It was also the first time he'd seen her in a suit—a beige jacket and a close-fitting dark brown skirt, and pumps. She smiled again and squeezed his arm, then sat back close to him.

He said, "You sure you don't want something to eat?"

"Yes, I'm sure—I had a very late lunch."

"If you tell me about your day," he said, "I'll tell you about mine."

"Oh God," she said, "my day. The copy machine broke down and I couldn't get it fixed until about four."

Charleen and her husband and two small children lived about fifteen miles from the city, in a restored farmhouse that was supposed to have been built a little after the Civil War. Though Charleen looked little of what she'd looked like then, Ben recognized her immediately—one of those kids at the luncheonette who rumor had lining up the high school football team, always smoking a cigarette and holding it by her side. The thin cheeks were gone; she was rounded and pleasant-looking. Her husband, a good-looking man with a beard, rode the train every day to the city, to some corporate position.

"I do remember you," she said. "You wrestled. I told Nancy your name was familiar." She smiled, pleased with herself. "Well, let me get the picture. I haven't looked at it in years."

The picture was long and unframed and a little cracked in places. The kids, about eighty of them, stood in four rows. In the center of the front row were Miss Pallington, the principal—old even then—and the vice principal, a woman Ben suddenly remembered as Mrs. O'Dare. Each of them, staring ahead stolidly, was holding an end of a pennant that said BAR-WYN—1972.

Charleen pointed to herself, laughing. Ben immediately saw George, then looked for his own picture—

he and Danny were together on the back row—and then saw, as he was searching for Julia, Ellen with a thin band around her straight blond hair.

"Where's Julia?" he asked.

Charleen's finger went to a girl on the third row. She was a little wisp of a thing, one of the few who weren't smiling. Though the face came back to him, the person didn't. He turned to Charleen.

"Do you remember if she was in our section?" The class had been divided into two sections. Charleen, he knew, had been in his, as had George and Ellen.

"Yes. I don't remember all that much about her, but I remember she was very shy. One reason you probably don't remember is that she didn't start out with us. She came, I think, in the fifth grade."

"I've been thinking about it," Nancy said. "I was in your class, the fifth, and she wasn't there. So it had to be the sixth."

"Then it was the sixth."

"You know what I remember most about her?" Charleen asked. "She had the most beautiful hand-writing."

Ben tried to remember. Something was beginning to stir. "Was she left-handed?"

"You're right," Charleen said, nodding. "I forgot."

Yes, he could see her now. Mostly it was at the blackboard—she used to write with her left elbow raised awkwardly. But the handwriting was beautiful. And something else—he was remembering something else. A composition she'd written. He remembered seeing that she had underlined some of the words in red ink. That wasn't unusual, but what had been un-usual to him, almost impossible—even though she'd used a ruler—was the way she underlined these words *twice*—the lines so thin and impossibly close, the ink never touching, never running together.

"It's such a pity," Charleen said. "And about George and Ellen. And all in a matter of a few weeks." She hadn't known about their deaths until Nancy had told her.

Ben looked from George's face to Ellen's to Julia's, then back, trying to think what in God's name those three kids could have had in common.

Or was it someone—could it be this?—out to wipe out the whole damn class?

He looked at the other faces, mostly the boys—he couldn't see a woman ever overpowering George Havers. He lingered over a few he hadn't liked, and those he'd been particularly friendly with; but most he remembered as just being around. He kept turning the picture over, where Charleen had collected about forty signatures. Most of the names he looked for didn't seem to be there. Or he just couldn't match them up with faces.

Charleen helped him remember some; he helped her with a few.

"I remember running around like crazy trying to get names," she said. "I don't think I have yours. No."

He was aware that Charleen and her husband were watching him as he kept studying the picture, that their curiosity was growing. They still didn't know why he wanted to see the picture.

He said, lowering it, "Look, I'm just very curious about something. And one is, as you say, that all this has happened in such a short time." He told them about his visit with Ellen, then about Ellen, George and Julia having been in the paper. "I don't know if their deaths are tied together," he said. "I can't help thinking so, but I don't know, I can't prove it."

"And you think," Charleen said, her face showing amazement, "maybe one of the kids has something to do with...?"

He gestured helplessly. "What I'm hoping to come up with," he said, "is something from the past, maybe an incident, a few incidents, maybe a kid's behavior that said this kid was going to be trouble, a psycho— anything I can turn over to the police and then leave it up to them."

"You know," she said, looking at him, "this is scary."

"I don't mean to scare you—I was worried about that but I don't know how else to say it."

She took the picture from him and looked at it again, very carefully. "I really can't think of a thing," she said, shaking her head. "I mean—just take Julia. I can't think of anyone hating *her*. I can't see anyone even remembering her." She shook her head again. "No."

"Can I ask you a favor? Can I borrow this for a few days?"

She looked at her husband, then back at him. "I guess so. Sure."

Her husband, obviously wanting to change the subject, asked if he could get anything for them—a drink? Tea? Coffee? No. Then the conversation turned to the age of the house. He began showing them around, what they'd done with the original hearth and beams, how this floor was the original stone, and how they'd bought replicas even of the original door handles. And as they all stood around smiling and admiring everything, he said to Ben, "Look, I've got to tell you. This is what's real." He pointed to the stone. "And that's real," pointing to a beam. "Do you know what I'm saying? I've just been listening, but I'm afraid that all this is going to do is make Charleen afraid to walk out in the dark. If you don't mind my saying, and please don't take it personally, I think it's all mule shit."

"I'm sorry," Ben said. "And you want to know the truth? I only hope you're right."

"Oh, Jim," Charleen said, looking up at him. And it was with a mild scolding tone, not anger—as if this was no way to treat company.

AS THEY PULLED AWAY from the house Nancy said, staring out her window, "I'm sorry he was so rude."

"No, don't be. I can understand it."

"I never knew him to be so rude," she said.

"Well, I just bring out the best in people." He thought she might smile, but she didn't; just kept staring out. He said, "You look tired."

"I am a little. I don't know why."

"You're letting all this upset you."

"No." She shook her head. "I don't know... maybe. But I've gotten a little tired."

In front of her house he turned off the motor and looked at her. She looked at him but didn't lift her face until he touched her cheek. He kissed her on the lips; she pressed against him, then put her cheek on his shoulder.

"Ben."

"Yes, Nan."

"Please understand." She was shaking her head. "I don't want to get involved."

"That's not hard to understand."

"And I am getting involved and I don't want to."

She said no more. But she remained in his arms a while longer. Then she squeezed him, then a little harder, and then let go.

WHILE MUCH OF his mind was still on Nancy, he called his niece when he got in the apartment, to see how she was and if she'd heard from her father. "Joannie, how are you, sweetheart?"

"Okay."

"You sure? You telling me the truth?"

"I'm telling the truth."

"I don't know whether you know it or not"—he felt a great need for her to know—"but I love you."

"I love you, too."

"Tell me, did you see your daddy?"

"Yes. He says he'll be home tomorrow."

"That's great."

She paused for a few moments, then said her grandmother wanted to talk with him.

"I forgot to mention this to you," Mrs. Chambers apologized. "I hate to act stupid, but is your middle name Evan?"

"Evan? No. Why?"

"Well, then I did no harm. I was pretty sure it wasn't." She told him about the call that came from a man wanting to know Dr. Newman's brother's phone number or address. "When I told him I couldn't give it out and asked if he wanted to leave a message, he asked was your middle name Evan. When I said it wasn't, he said oh, that's who he was really looking for."

The phone down, Ben sat for several moments looking at it. Though it was an unusual call, it didn't seem all *that* unusual—until he remembered his picture in the paper with Harry. And that the story had given only Harry's address.

all teams, football—whether someone made the picture in and posed with Harry. And that one story has never early 1970s nowhere.

EIGHTEEN

BEN JUST SAT THERE for a few moments, trying to think what else it might have been. Like, maybe the guy had really been looking for another Ben Newman. But no. Too much of a coincidence that he'd called so soon after that picture was in the paper. And even that he'd called Harry, the only one of them named in the story.

No, it was someone who recognized him, then called to make sure and gave a phony middle name.

But why him now? Why George and Ellen and Julia? Why them and now him?

Unless, as he'd been thinking, it was the entire class. After all these years, some crazy out to kill all of them!

He looked at the picture again, aware how hard he was breathing. But he managed to calm down as he ran his finger slowly along the rows of faces.

Who, out of all these kids? Which of the kids he might have played ball with, war, King of the Hill, gone sledding with?

His finger kept moving, pausing, moving. He remembered all their faces, but still couldn't recall most of their full names, even some first names. He kept flipping over to the back, but Charleen had gotten mostly the girls' names.

It was even hard to remember a lot of them as they were back then. There were those handful of guys he'd known real well, nice kids, but most of the others had just been faces in class or in the schoolyard. Even the few he hadn't liked, had even had some fistfights with, none stood out now as an *enemy,* someone who—

He stopped at Cookie, the guy Danny said had an auto repair shop in Barwyn.

Ben couldn't remember his real name, it was always Cookie except in class—a short, weaselly, black-haired kid. And thinking of Cookie made him think of someone else—and he looked for him, a kid Cookie used to pal around with. And there he was on the back row, tall, thin-faced, hands on his hips and his body crooked to one side, grinning crookedly, too. Ben couldn't recall his name, just that he'd been a god-damn creep.

IN THE MORNING, Ben started to call his old friend Dan, hesitated, then lowered the phone. Dan thought he was out of his mind as it was; and now to go back and say it wasn't the bicentennial after all, and which of these kids did he think could be out to kill the whole class?

Who else might know something? Might remember some of the names he still didn't know? Might even come up with things about them, back then or even now?

He took another long look at the picture. Then he opened the drawer for the phone book, began flipping the pages. Good, it was under the name Cookie. Cookie's Auto Repair.

It felt a little bizarre, thinking of talking to Cookie.

He couldn't remember the two of them even saying one word to each other all through school.

A man answered the phone. "Yes, Cookie's here, hold on."

Cookie came on. "Yeah."

"Cookie, my name's Ben Newman. I knew you a long time ago; I went to school with you. I wonder if I could see you for a few minutes today."

"Ben who?"

"Newman."

"Ben Newman," he repeated thoughtfully. "Don't remember offhand. But I'll be here. All day."

Ten minutes later Ben was walking through his apartment's lobby. The glass doors, he could see ahead, opened to a dazzle of sunshine. He was aware, approaching them, how safe he felt in here, in a building with security, in an apartment with an unlisted phone.

But the streets had become starkly different from before. They weren't safe for him anymore.

COOKIE'S GARAGE was on a side street, set back in a courtyard cluttered with cars and wrecks and old parts. He was standing outside one of the bays as Ben drove in. He must have gained a hundred pounds—the pinched little face had become thick and jowly.

He was watching something in the bay. Although he'd glanced over briefly as Ben got out he didn't pay any more attention to him. Ben stood near him, waiting. Cookie kept looking in there, at someone working under a car on a lift. Ben had the feeling he liked to keep people waiting.

"Cookie?" Cookie turned slowly, said nothing. "I'm Ben Newman. I called you a little while ago?"

Cookie's face showed no expression. He just looked at him. Then, still studying him, he said, "You look sorta familiar. The name's sorta familiar."

"Well, it goes way back. Maybe this'll help." Ben took the picture out of a manila envelope. Cookie wiped his hands on his pants before taking it.

"Jesus Christ," he said after a moment, still without expression, "I ain't seen this thing in years. Jesus Christ, where am I?" Then, "Oh, shit." He smiled for the first time, looking at himself. Then he looked at Ben. "Where're you? Oh, sure," Cookie said then. "Oh, Christ." He kept looking at the picture, then looking at Ben. "So what can I do for you?"

"I'm trying to locate as many of the kids as I can, particularly the guys, and I heard you were still in Barwyn and I thought maybe you could help. I don't even remember a lot of the names."

"Jee-zus, I don't know." He started to look at the picture again when one of his men came up and asked if the parts for the Olds had come in. "Christ," Cookie said, "they didn't come in?" He headed for the office, the two of them trailing after him. He made a long angry call, then after his man left it was a few moments before Cookie seemed to remember what Ben wanted. And suddenly he sounded annoyed. "I don't know, I don't know where anyone lives—maybe a couple, a few. Names—I don't know."

He pointed out several whose names Ben still didn't recognize, then one he now remembered. "You gotta've read about him. A little twerp. Gary Piatrozik. He's in the mayor's office."

"What's this guy's name?" Ben asked, pointing to the kid standing crookedly with his hands on his hips.

"Oh, him," Cookie said with a grin. "Karl. Karl Jubb."

Of course. Everyone had called him Jubb. The two pals, Jubb and Cookie.

Ben asked, "Do you know where he lives?"

"Naah," Cookie said, shaking his head. "Last I heard of Jubb was about ten years ago—he was supposed to be living somewhere near Pittsburgh, and he was supposed to have embezzled a lot of money." Then Cookie, pointing at Ellen, said indifferently, "Remember this broad? You know she's dead?"

"Yes. I know she died. That's something I wanted to talk to you about." Then, pointing, "You remember George Havers? Do you know he died? A few weeks before Ellen?"

Cookie looked at George. "Yeah?" Then his expression went sour. "He was a guy thought he was such a goddamn big shot. A real big man." He handed back the picture and looked at one of his men who'd come in from the adjoining bay. The fellow showed him a part he was having a problem with, and Cookie walked out with him and stood watching as he leaned under a hood. From a distant bay came the bluish flash of a welding torch.

"Come on, what the fuck you doin'?" Cookie suddenly exclaimed. "Gimme the goddamn thing." He bent over the engine, began working, then rose up after a few minutes. "For Christ's sake," he muttered. He watched his man for a while, then instead of returning to the office he went outside the bay and stood looking around. He picked up something from the ground, looked at it absently, threw it away. He walked over to one of the other bays and looked in.

More, Ben was sure, of the making-you-wait bit.

The ringing of the phone, like an alarm through the yard, brought Cookie back. He talked for at least ten minutes, standing, his back to Ben, about hunting and a new rifle he'd bought. By then a customer pulled up in a pickup truck, but Cookie wasn't in a hurry about him either. It was about five more minutes before he went out to the fellow, and after looking under his hood he came back to the office and took down a thick loose-leaf manual from a shelf. He put it on his desk, opened it, then glanced up at Ben. "Look," he said, "this is a bad time. But I really don't know anything more about the kids. You wanna come back, though, you wanna call—you know, I'm here."

"I'll see," Ben said. Cookie immediately began going through the manual, turning the pages over the large rings. "Good seeing you," Ben said to his bent head. He watched him for a few moments more, then started to walk out. But something stopped him at the door—a large newspaper ad, Scotch-taped to the glass.

It was a half-page ad for the garage. And looking out from it, smiling, was Cookie's face. Ben could see that it was from the Barwyn *Reporter,* but there was no date.

"Cookie," he called, "when did this run?"

Cookie looked up long enough to say, "This week. I been running 'em two, three years now." Then he showed the customer something in the manual.

Ben kept looking at him. Then he turned and walked quickly to his car.

He stopped at the first public phone, got City Hall's number from Information and asked for Gary Piatrozik. The woman who answered said he was at a meeting. No, Ben said, no message.

He hung up slowly.

He'd found out what he wanted to for now.

Piatrozik had been getting quite a bit of publicity as an aide to the mayor. And he was alive, as was Cookie, even with his face in the paper every week for years. As was Dan, with the sign HAUPT on his store, and just about everyone in their class knowing it was his family's business. Why not them? Why just some of the class—including him?

NINETEEN

IN THE CAR, Ben sat tensely, staring ahead. Somehow it would make some kind of horrendous sense if it was the whole class, if someone carried a hatred for all of them over the years. It would even make some kind of sense if it was just, say, he and George and maybe a few of the other guys. They'd at least done something together, played ball together, been friends. But Ellen?—he didn't think he'd even *talked* to her in grammar school. And Julia?

They'd all been in the same section, but so were Dan and Cookie and Gary Piatrozik.

So it must be something that *happened* or that someone back then *thought* had happened.

He tried to sort out the classes he and George and Ellen and Julia had been in together, the teachers they'd had. Up through the sixth grade—when Julia had come to school—each of the two sections had one teacher all day. Then from the seventh through the eighth, Barwyn became a kind of junior high. Each section had a homeroom teacher and the kids would go as a group to various other teachers.

There was Nevon in eighth grade, for homeroom and social studies. But who else in eighth? Oaks— Mrs. Oaks, for math. But damn if he could think of anyone else.

Seventh. Cassaway—how could he forget Catherine Cassaway?—for homeroom and English. Oaks, too, for math. And Winders—Winders for history.

He knew he would think of others, probably most of them, once he stopped trying so hard. Right now there was a whirl of faces and names that he couldn't put in any specific class. Like with sixth grade. Shumlin taught one of the sections, but who else?

He went back to the phone, deciding to try Nevon again. Maybe, just maybe, something had happened or there'd been something about one of the kids, such as a history of emotional problems, that only the teachers knew about. Ben called the high school.

"Can I leave a message for Mr. Nevon?"

"Hold on." But when the woman came back: "He's not in today and we're not sure when he'll be in, but if you'd like to leave it anyway…"

"I see; I'll call back."

He wanted to find out first if he could reach him at home.

Nevon answered the phone, his voice sounding more gravelly than usual.

"Who?" Nevon said when Ben gave his name.

"Ben Newman. I was over to see you at school?"

"Oh. Sure. The writin' man."

"I hate to bother you at home," Ben said, "you sound like you're not feeling well. But something else has come up and I was wondering if you might be able to give me a little time again."

"Well…" Nevon said, giving it some thought. "Well, look, if you have a thing for germs, whenever you want."

NEVON LIVED ON a narrow street of fashionably old, stone or stucco single homes. He came to the door in his robe, pajamas and slippers, his thick, slightly graying black hair uncombed. He gave a couple of little coughs into his fist, then motioned for Ben to follow him into the den, richly colored with throw rugs, prints and the spines of hundreds of books. "Don't breathe on me," he said, pointing Ben to a chair. "I don't want to get well me, and have to go back." He took a rocking chair and sat with his right leg across his knee. "So."

"I really appreciate this."

"Look, I want to be written up, I'll do anything. So," he said again, then: "You say it's about something else."

"Well, it's about the same thing," Ben said, leaning forward, hands folded between his knees, "except for one thing. The deaths have nothing to do with the bicentennial after all. Let me show you something."

He brought over the picture, handed it to Nevon and crouched next to him.

"Oh my," Nevon said, pointing to the principal and vice principal. "You have beautified my day." Miss Pallington, the principal had died, he said, and Mrs. O'Dare retired. "Oh," he said shortly, "here's you. I was right, I remember you."

"Do you remember this girl?" Ben said, pointing. "Julia Neubauer?"

Nevon looked at her carefully. "I remember the face but I don't really remember anything about her."

"She died Saturday night," Ben said. "It was a hit-and-run."

"Really," he said, frowning. His face had become serious for the first time.

"That makes her the third person in this same class

who's died within the past few weeks. And each of them died violently. And there was always something about them in the paper just before they died.'' Nevon looked at him. Ben said, ''I know this was a long time ago but I wonder if you'd try something for me. Here's George Havers,'' he went on, pointing, ''here's Ellen, and here's Julia. Can you possibly think of anything back then that someone, some nut, might think they had in common? And, not so coincidentally, had in common with me?''

''You?''

''I don't want to sound dramatic but I've got a good reason to think so.''

''Christ, have you told the cops?''

''Not about me yet, because I don't know if they believe any of it. But I will. I was hoping maybe to have something else to give them.''

Nevon looked at him sternly, then at the picture. After a few moments: ''Look, I'm sorry, I can't think of anything.''

''Well, was there anything about any of the kids, particularly the boys, that might make you think they might be behind it? I'm not asking you necessarily to tell me. But if there was something, please, I urge you, go to the cops with it.''

Nevon immediately glowered, waved a hand in front of his face. ''Look, I'm not going to get involved in anything like that. No way. I—'' But he looked at the picture again. ''Most of the kids I only know from their faces, but they all strike me as having been good kids. Almost all my kids are good. I find that if you treat kids good—'' He paused. He seemed to be hesitating about something, then said, ''Look, I'm going to level with you. There are only two kids in this class

I remember I didn't like." He pointed to Cookie and Jubb. "And though I'm not proud of it, I'll tell you how much I disliked them. I'm talking too much but I'll tell you. Remember that retarded youngster, something happened to, there was that big thing about?"

It was several moments before it came back to Ben, the only dark incident he could remember of those days in Barwyn. A thin little girl about his age, who only made sounds and giggled a lot, lived with an obese mother right across the street from the school. And sometimes you'd see her standing clutching the schoolyard fence, staring in; and once, he remembered, she came in and began chasing balls kids missed, until some of the kids yelled at her to get out of there—some were always making fun of her—and her mother came from the house and brought her back across the street, clutching her hand and yelling at her. Then one day when he was in the sixth or seventh grade—seventh—kids, not all, he hadn't been one of them, began getting called to the principal's office, and the stories started going around that something happened to Betsie—that was her name; after all these years, Betsie—that something happened but no one knew what.

The stories the kids told went from rape, to someone having put it in her mouth, to she'd only had paint poured all over her, to someone had just tied her up or even only scared her in some way. But whatever it was, soon there was a FOR SALE sign on the lawn, and that was the end of Betsie.

"Well, they're the only kids I even thought could have done it," Nevon was saying. "When I heard of it they just jumped into my head, and then I was a little ashamed of it. It was my own bias after all. But it shows you what I thought of them. Anyway, I know Edwin''—Cookie's real name—''has turned out very well. I don't know about the other kid, but with my skill at prediction he's probably a missionary in Africa.''

"You know if they ever found out who did it?''
"No.''

"What did happen? We heard all sorts of stories.''

"All I know,'' Nevon said, ''is that she'd been found running out of the woods, moaning, her wrists tied together and either one or both shoes off and mud all over her face and in her hair. Since she was so retarded she wasn't able to give a clue to what happened or who did it, but they did know she wasn't raped. They couldn't even prove she was sexually molested, but her clothes were so messed up that the police felt she'd somehow broken free or her abductor had been scared off before it could happen. But look, you got me talking and I'm off talking,'' Nevon said. "Kids might not even have had anything to do with that, in fact, they questioned all the ones they thought might have, so forget what I said. And I know the cops were looking for some old guy... I don't know if they ever found him. Anyway,'' he said, handing back the picture, ''that's all I know, which you can keep out of my biography.''

"Do you know,'' Ben asked, ''which of the other sixth-to-eighth-grade teachers are still at the school?''

"Well, if you want to talk to someone,'' Nevon said, "I'd say your best bet is Shumlin. He used to teach sixth, you know. And he's the principal now.''

"Do you think he'd be hard to approach?''

"I don't think so. Milt's a nice guy. And he likes to talk. Especially to kids who've made good.''

"Can I use your name?"

Nevon looked at him thoughtfully. "I'll tell you what. I'll call him." He left the room for about fifteen minutes. When he came back he said, "He wanted to know what it was about and I had to tell him."

"Fine."

"He thinks he remembers you. Do you have a sister?"

"No."

"Don't tell him. He can see you at a quarter to four."

A FEW CHILDREN were still drifting out of the gray, rough-stone building as he parked near the main gate. Some were shooting baskets in the yard or just chasing one another around. It felt even stranger walking across this yard and up the worn steps than it had at the high school. And where the high school hadn't appeared as small as he thought it would, here it was as if he'd stepped into a miniature world.

The foyer felt dark, though it was lighted, but once he walked into the corridor the school became far brighter than he recalled. The corridors were beige— he remembered them as green, though he wasn't sure—and the rooms he passed were light and colorful. The desks, so little, had a modern Scandinavian look; they used to be a darkish-redwood, and certainly there'd been no chrome.

Again, as at the high school, he had no idea where the office was. A young teacher—surely some of his had been this young, and Miss Kramer, for one, had been even more attractive—stopped long enough to smile and point the way.

He'd forgotten about Miss Kramer. Third grade.

And now he thought of Miss Dougherty, in fifth, so fat she had to walk sideways through the classroom door; and of Mrs. Wilson, who played piano during assembly. He'd never had her, nor had he ever been lucky enough to have sexy Miss Blake who he used to fantasize holding him in her long, bracelet-jingling arms when he was no more than nine.

He remembered Shumlin very clearly and was a little surprised to find that he had only aged, not changed. His head, always glossy bald, was fringed with gray now, but his mustache was still mostly black. Tall, slender, he had a severe look, which he rarely altered with more than a tenuous smile; but Ben didn't remember him as a severe teacher.

They shook hands and Shumlin motioned him to a chair, then sat, swiveled slightly and leaning back behind his desk. "Yes, yes, I had the feeling I sort of remembered," he said, studying him. "So you're a writer. Wayne tells me you wrote a successful book and you write articles. That's wonderful. Wonderful."

"You look very well," Ben said. "I'd recognize you in a second."

"Ah. Can I ask you something?" Shumlin asked. "It's something I'm interested in. When you first, you know, wanted to write, did your parents object?"

Ben was a little surprised at the question. "They didn't really object, no. But they couldn't see any reason I couldn't do it on the side, like after I finished surgery for the day."

"You know what I wanted to be?" Shumlin said quietly after a few moments. "An astronomer. And I'd have made a good one. But there wasn't any money for dreams; my father had a tailor shop, and there were seven of us kids, so if I was going to col-

lege I had to take up something where I could get a
secure job fast. Teaching was very honorable—I think
more honorable then than now. And my parents were
very proud. But let me tell you something, it was very
hard those days. Some of my friends, I used to have
a lot of fancy friends, they could understand teaching—but grammar school? What's that for a man?
They didn't know I didn't need an M.A. then.''

Suddenly he seemed a little flustered, as if he'd
opened up too much. ''But I've been very happy
here,'' he said quickly, nodding. ''I wouldn't change
it. I not only have my M.A., I've got my doctorate.
And the school—we still don't have a lot of the problems other schools have. The kids are nice—by and
large they're all very nice—the parents are nice, the
community is nice. It's held up fairly well. The
school's stayed pretty solid, even though it's got a
much better mix now. Anyway,'' he said, leaning
back, ''I don't want to take up much more of your
time. Wayne told me the story. And I think it's only
fair for me to tell you it's very, *very* hard for me to
believe.''

''I can't say I blame you.''

Looking at the class picture now, Shumlin said,
''Yes, I remember George and Ellen, and I think I
remember Julia, too. I remember them as very, very
nice.'' He looked at Ben. ''It's like I see them today.
What a pity. Such young people.'' He started to turn
to the picture again, but looked back at Ben. ''As I
say, Wayne told me what you want, and I've got to
tell you that as far as picking out kids, I can't do that.
Well, I'm not going to do that. These were *children.*
Anyway,'' giving the picture a slow, sweeping look,

"I don't see anything that jumps out at me. All I see, like I say, are kids. No," he said, handing it back.

"Dr. Shumlin, that incident back then," Ben said, "the incident with the retarded girl across the street—do you know if it was ever solved?"

Shumlin stared at him, almost in disbelief "My God, what are you trying to do? I don't know if it was solved, maybe it was, I don't know. I don't even know what happened. All I know is the police were here, it wasn't any of the kids here. That's all I know. My God, you really are digging things up!"

"I'm not trying to upset you."

"I'm not upset, I'm not upset! But I'm sorry, I can't help you, I can't think of a thing. And if the police come, I can't help them either. I just don't know anything."

Ben asked which of the teachers he had in the sixth, seventh and eighth grades were still at the school.

"Just three," Shumlin said, obviously annoyed. "Miss Cassaway, Mrs. Oaks, and Miss Hendricks," whom Ben had forgotten but who was on sabbatical anyway.

"Is it all right with you," Ben asked, "if I talk to them?"

"It's a free country, I can't stop you—why would I stop you? But I can't give you their home phone numbers. You'll have to get them elsewhere or reach them here."

"Would it be okay if I try their rooms now?"

"No, they're gone," Shumlin said quickly, with a wave of his hand. And something immediately became clear to Ben: that the only reason Shumlin had seen him was to try to end this, to keep it from growing into a scandal.

And that Shumlin wanted to talk to the teachers first.

TWENTY

HARRY CALLED HIM in the morning. "I just want you to know I'm out of there."

"Great. Where are you?"

"At the office. I even saw a patient at the hospital." He sounded manic, as if a drug were working on him. "I'm fine, heart's fine. Had a case of nerves. Enough of this bullshit."

"Good."

"I just got a call from a goddamn reporter, heard I was out and wants to see me. Can you imagine—I'm out five minutes and they already know about it! Anyway, I almost told him," he said, his voice compressed with anger, "ask me whatever the fuck you want, go on ask me."

"What did you say?"

"I had nothing to say." He took a long breath. "But it's hard to keep quiet; I don't know if my lawyer's right. It's like I've got something to hide. You know what really hit me in the hospital? I didn't do anything!" A fresh fierceness came into his voice. "I didn't do anything, the sons of bitches. I made a mistake and I'm sorry, God knows I'm sorry, but I didn't do anything."

"Harry, I know." But it was as if Harry hadn't heard.

"Nothing, didn't do anything! But I'm walking around with this—this conscience like I did it. You know something? I've been thinking it out. Why that lie detector, why didn't it really say anything? Ben," and he tried to lower his voice, "I was going around feeling inside like I did it. Pat, me—we used to have fights, sure. But who doesn't, right? One of our biggest fights—you know what it was about? You won't believe. It was over a nonsense. It started with I couldn't find certain socks. Would you believe?"

"Harry, we all do things like that, say things we don't mean. You're using it to beat yourself the hell up."

"No more. That's what I mean. I was just saying. Everything was up in my head. It's like I was really guilty, I deserved whatever happened. But I don't. I don't need to hide in a hospital and I don't need to get chest pains. I'm not afraid to talk to the goddamn police. My lawyer can go fuck himself. They can all go fuck themselves."

"Harry," he said, "how about us getting together today? How about, say, for lunch?"

"No. You think I'm not okay?"

"I didn't say that, Harry. Lunch, I'm just saying lunch. And you know what? I haven't seen your new office."

"We'll do it sometime. But I'm okay! I'm fine! And I've got a million things to do and I'm sure so do you."

Ben wanted to say, "Oh, fuck you!" and just let the phone drop from two feet up. He wanted to say, "Harry, I've got problems of my own, I've got someone after me I don't want to worry you about," but instead he said, "Okay, we'll talk, you take it easy," and hung up.

He sat for a while, pushed away from his desk, then opened the Philly phone book he'd been looking through, and continued looking for Karl Jubb. Getting nowhere, he looked this time for Miss Cassaway and Mrs. Oaks.

There was no Cassaway but there was an Oaks, P. He had no idea what the eighth grade teacher's first name was but he recognized the address as in Barwyn. He called the number but there was no answer. He would try her later.

He flipped the pages of the book, then called the elementary school.

"Would you take a message for me? Would you have Miss Cassaway call me at this number?"

CATHERINE CASSAWAY watched as the children came into the classroom from the noisy corridor, each of them suddenly silent. It was the last class of the day. Occasionally her stare followed them until they sat down, then it went back to the door. A few of them looked at her quickly as they entered, then away. She waited until the exact minute, then went to the door and closed it.

She came back to her desk and lifted up the attendance sheet. She looked from face to face, name to face—she didn't have to call roll; she could tell who was missing—then said, "Matthew Walters?" She addressed it to Evelyn Tolson on the third row, though she could have asked anyone. But she had taught Evelyn's mother and, like her mother, she was one of the ones you could trust.

"He reported out sick, Miss Cassaway. He wasn't in any of the classes."

She put down the sheet. She wanted to grab up the pile of compositions on her desk but had almost lost her voice with the previous class, and decided to hold off, to distribute them at the end with just her written comments. Except for Evelyn—and *hers* wasn't all that good this time—but except for Evelyn and Sam Wendt and maybe one other, they ranged from intolerable to mediocre.

She picked up a little stack of three-by-five cards, each with the name of a pupil. She took off the rubber band and stood facing the class. This, she'd learned long ago, was much more effective than having them raise their hands to questions—only the good ones did it, after all. And her slow picking of a card kept them attentive, glued.

"I can't believe," she said, "I really can't, that I have to go back and teach you the principal parts of verbs." She looked around, then at her cards. She picked one at random, looked at it, then up.

"Peter."

He stood up by his desk. She was almost sorry who it was. He would know.

"Give us the principal parts of verbs."

"Infinitive. Past tense. Past participle."

"Infinitive, past tense, past participle," she repeated when he sat down. "All right. Now regular verbs." She drew another card. "Courtney Swift." There were two Courtneys. "How do we form the past tense and past participle of most regular verbs?"

Courtney drew in her lip. "We add…'ed'?"

"I'm asking you, don't ask me."

"We add 'ed,'" she said quickly.

"All right," Catherine Cassaway said, "Irregular verbs. Here's a list of verbs with irregular parts we should all know." She went to the blackboard and quickly wrote down a row of verbs, leaving space for the past tense and past participle.

A card. "William Ross. The first one." He went to the board, got it right: ride, rode, ridden.

"Janice. Next word." Oh, God. Wring, wrung, wrang. "Sit down." Another quick card. "Elizabeth."

Elizabeth erased "wrang" and replaced it with "wrung." She kept looking at Miss Cassaway and didn't start back to her seat until Miss Cassaway turned and glared at Janice before snapping up other card.

Now, at last, it was ten to three, just time enough to assign homework and to have Evelyn go up and down the aisles to hand back compositions. The bell, and they were rising now, like a horde, and her stiffened head and stare didn't quiet them this time; it never did the last class of the day. As usual, a couple of them lingered behind to ask questions but they were sensible questions for the most part, thank God, these were the all-too-rare kind of young people who made it rewarding.

On her way out of the building she checked her box in the office to see if there were any memos. There was a note. Frowning, she tried to think who was this Benjamin Newman she was supposed to call. Then she saw Milton Shumlin looking at her from the doorway to his office in the rear. He motioned for her to wait.

She was proud of herself that she'd never once envied him his promotion—not outwardly, anyway—although so many of the others did. All she'd ever wanted was to be a teacher, but she would have liked to have at least been asked.

"Miss Cassaway, I just want to mention something. Someone said he might be calling you, and it's very strange and I don't want you to think I told him to."

"A Mr. Newman?"

"Oh, he called? Well, it is something very strange and I think you ought to know."

Walking out to her car she felt bewildered and annoyed. She knew, of course, of one of the deaths, poor Ellen, but she barely remembered George Havers, and she didn't this Julia-whatever, at all. And Newman—she thought she remembered a Benjamin Newman but wasn't sure.

Anyway, what did any of this have to do with her?

FROM HER APARTMENT at the top of the stairs, the elderly woman watched the thin black-haired man climbing up, her 23-inch TV dead-weight in his hands. He set it on a stand and gave her the bill. Then he unwrapped the cord and looked around for a socket.

"I could have gotten a new set for this," she said, looking at the bill.

He resisted a quick look at her—he might spit. He'd told her that when he'd taken it out, the old bitch, don't give him that now! He plugged in the cord and turned on the set, then adjusted it. He tried every channel. He stood up from one knee and looked at her. She tried it herself.

"You sure you put in the same thing, not a cheap one?" she asked. "I mean, you did it yourself? You know for sure?"

"Yeah." He nodded.

"You know," she said suddenly, "I don't know if I have a check. Where're my checks?"

His stare followed her out of the room. He could hear her in the next room, mumbling.

He didn't care if she had a check, didn't have a check, if he had to carry the damn thing down again, all he wanted was out of here. Each stop was getting worse, each stop was forever.

She was coming out with a check now, wrote it out painfully. "You got a cold?" she asked.

She must have seen his hands. The shaking was getting harder to control.

He didn't answer. He took the check but didn't put it in his wallet until he was walking down the stairs. The trembling was much less when no one was looking.

In the small truck, he looked at his next stops. He was finding it harder to concentrate.

He'd been outside the doctor's house half the night last night, and there was almost no point going back there just to wait, to look. It might be forever before Ben Newman showed up again.

But what was building up in his head, what kept growing: just get someone from the house, grab someone, choke them or break each finger until they told!

TWENTY-ONE

THAT AFTERNOON someone, a man, finally answered the phone at the number listed for an Oaks, P. "Yes," he told Ben, "Mrs. Oaks teaches at Barwyn Elementary. And, yes, she's home." But it was taking forever for her to come to the phone. Then the man came back on. "May I tell her who's calling?"

"My name's Ben Newman. I was in her class a number of years ago."

There was a brief pause, then a hesitant, "She's—a little busy right now. And she's going out. I don't know when she'll be back."

Though Ben left his number he was sure he would never hear from her, that Shumlin must have spoken with her and she didn't want to get involved.

A little later though, when he had to go out for a while, he came back to find his answering machine blinking. For a few moments he thought he'd been wrong about Oaks. But he hadn't been. It made no difference though.

"This is Miss Cassaway. I will call again later."

SOMEHOW IT WAS even harder visualizing talking to her, seeing her, than it was Shumlin. And certainly much more than Oaks, a little woman with an easy smile. Cassaway was mythical, even back then.

Though he could remember only certain things about her, they stood out clearly. That face with the tight, black hair. Those goddamn three-by-five cards, the way she'd pick one and look at it and then, while everyone was hoping and praying it wasn't them, how she'd look around the room as if she didn't know after all this time where the kid was sitting, and then say the name.

And the terror most of all—those stern eyes that could melt you in terror.

It was about an hour later that the call came through. "Is this Mr. Newman?" God, how that voice was the same, though it seemed to have lost a trace of its firmness.

"Yes. Miss Cassaway, thanks so much for returning my call. I used to be in your class—"

"Yes," she interrupted, "Dr. Shumlin told me. I've been thinking and I think I remember your name. Dr. Shumlin told me something about what you want and I must say"—she sounded impatient now, annoyed—"I can't imagine what you'd want from me."

"I wonder if you could just give me a little of your time. I'd like to tell you for myself what's been happening."

"I don't know." She sounded even more annoyed. "We've got a teachers' meeting tomorrow, I..." She paused, then, "I don't know. How long will this take?"

"Whatever time you can give me."

Silence. "Well..." He could just see that exasperated look. "If you can get to my house by five."

Setting down the phone, his first quick thought was: why's she seeing me? Why, when Shumlin... And yet that was probably a big part of the reason, if not all of it. That no one was going to tell her what to do!

And he was aware of how tense—more than tense, how goddamn tense—she'd made him.

DRIVING TO HER HOUSE he remembered how his whole body used to tighten as he approached her classroom. Yet he'd never had trouble with her, she'd never had reason to even give him that stare, let alone one of her scathing dressing-downs or a whirl of her pointed finger to "get yourself into the cloak room or to the principal's office—fast, faster." In fact, she often used to call on him to do things for her—distribute papers or open or close the windows, using that long pole that reached to the top. And he always got decent marks. But there was always that feeling that at any moment she could turn on you.

He was entering Barwyn now, past the corner a block from his house.

Cassaway, kids in the other seventh grade homeroom would gloat. Bad enough having her for English, let alone homeroom. Yet a few kids, girls as he remembered, were proud about saying they loved her. And there were a couple of kids, Jubb especially, that he absolutely used to marvel at because they didn't seem to give a damn, used to be able to stand there next to their desks time after time with a swallowed grin, looking to the side at other kids while she just about lifted the skin off them.

It was hard to believe that not only would he be seeing her as an adult but in her *home.* What could have been more impossible than to be in Miss Cassaway's home?

Pulling up to the curb he recalled a few times as a

kid when he'd actually avoided this part of this block because it might mean meeting her. And here he was, walking up her steps.

He expected her to look somewhat the same, yet was a little startled when she opened the door and he saw how much she did—the same coiled-back hair, though gray now; the same severe look.

He smiled. "Miss Cassaway, I'm Ben Newman."

She said nothing, just stood looking at him, her face expressionless. Then she nodded slightly and said, "Come in." She left the door partly open and looked at him again, carefully. "Yes," she said quietly, "I remember you."

"That's nice to hear. I've thought of you a lot over the years."

Her expression still didn't change. And suddenly it made him remember that whenever she did smile—a rare, rare flicker of a smile—you could almost feel relief sweep through the class.

"And I remember your class quite well," she said. "When Dr. Shumlin told me what you wanted I tried to think who was in it—I knew Ellen was, she went to my church. What I'm saying is I remember it as a good class. So this is shocking."

"Miss Cassaway, I know it sounds absolutely crazy. After all, it was years ago, we were kids. I know that. But I'm convinced someone in that class is behind all this. Or if he wasn't actually in the class he had something against some of the kids who were."

"I'm sorry," she said, shaking her head, her jaws firm. "I have no idea about anything like that. I really shouldn't have put you to this trouble—but I'm afraid I was curious. I'm sorry, but I really have nothing to say."

"Can I ask one thing of you? Would you at least look at this for me?" He drew part of the class picture from the envelope, then when she didn't object he took it out and handed it to her.

Looking at it she sat down on the sofa. "I don't know what you want me…" But she kept looking at it, in a way that made it obvious she hadn't really remembered most of the children until now.

Ben, sitting in a nearby chair, watched her, then his gaze drifted momentarily past her to the end table. On it was an oval-framed photo, tinted, of a woman who vaguely resembled Miss Cassaway with a girl of about twelve who he realized actually was Miss Cassaway. Another picture of her mother, an even older one, was on the mantel near an antique, bronze clock. The sofa was a dark velvety blue, with two rectangles of lace as head rests.

"Yes," she said, still looking at it, "this was a good class. Here's poor Ellen, and George—I remember George so well. And here you are, Benjamin."

"Miss Cassaway, can I ask you about Julia Neubauer? Do you remember her at all?"

From Miss Cassaway's look, she didn't; she was even having trouble finding her. Ben came over and pointed to her.

"Of course," she said, annoyed at herself. "She was a very nice young girl. Very nice, very quiet."

"Did you know she died, too? This past Saturday night?"

She frowned, then looked at Julia again. "Dr. Shumlin mentioned something…"

"Would you happen to remember anything else about her? Is there anything, say, that might connect her in your mind with Ellen, with George—"

"No." She shook her head. "No. She was just very nice, and so were Ellen and George. There were a number of nice children—smart." She pointed to a boy whose name, Ben recalled, was Alan Green, a kid who'd had a special distinction: he'd lived next door to her. "A wonderful child. No, this was a very good class. You're wrong," she said, suddenly indignant. "There's not a one here... They rarely so much as spoke out of turn in those days, they did their work, they listened."

All of them? He was trying to conceal his astonishment. She forgot? Cookie, whom she'd almost hit with her fist that time? And Jubb—she could look at Jubb's face and say that? There'd been talk that if his father hadn't been something in the Democratic party he wouldn't have just been suspended a couple of times, he'd have been expelled.

"Times were different," she said, "you just don't know. Some children were mischievous, but they weren't—I'll call it evil. Today, drugs..."

As if there'd been absolutely none then—he knew for sure of one time a teacher found grass in the boys' room. And though drugs didn't really happen until high school, he'd known of a few of the older kids who were doing it.

"It's drugs," she said, "they talk filth. I don't let it happen in my classes, but some of these teachers... Things have changed." She stopped, seemed to be struggling whether to say something. "It's—a little bit in the change of population. And I don't mean just racial. People are moving out, a lot of the fine old families. It's not the same. They're trying, there's a bicentennial celebration, but it can never be like the old days. No,'' she said, standing up, "this was a good class.''

She started to hand the picture back to him, then stopped, frowning. He watched as she looked at it again. Then she shook her head slowly. "No,'' she said, but it was more to herself than to him, "I forgot. He didn't graduate. I forgot he was even in that class.'' She looked at Ben, still frowning. "What was his name? Leo… No, Leopold.''

He said nothing, kept waiting.

"Leopold,'' she said. "And it was something like…Arra. Something like Arra or Assa.''

An image was beginning to form in his mind. But that had been a pathetic kid more than anything else, just about a stereotype of a kid kids pick on, with a sunken chin and snot edging his wide nostrils half the time.

"Azza,'' she said. "That's right. Leopold Azza. A dreadful child.''

But Ben couldn't picture him as dreadful, just pathetic.

"You know,'' she said, "maybe I shouldn't say this. But I know you asked about it. And I forgot he was in your class. But that little girl? That poor little retarded girl? The one all those horrible things were done to? I don't know if you even remember. But the only one I could think might have done it was him. I wouldn't have put it past him. I even saw him playing with her once in the yard.''

Again Betsie. First, Jubb and Cookie, and now Leopold?

"I really shouldn't say this,'' she said. "But I even told the police and I heard they questioned him.

But..." She gestured. "I don't know what happened. All I know is he left in the eighth grade."

MISS CASSAWAY swept hanger after hanger along the rod in her closet, searching for the right sweater, then stopped, annoyed she was letting herself be upset. But she couldn't help it. She should never have let him come over. It was tragic that young people should die, but to try to trace it back to something that happened in one of *her* classes? Nonsense, it was nonsense!

All he'd accomplished doing, all she'd let him do, was intrude into her life. He'd even stirred up that...that Leopold in her mind again. Though she wouldn't swear to this day that he hadn't done that to that child, he'd become pretty much blended over the years into all the Leopold-types she'd had since; sometimes it seemed that God gave her at least one every year.

She found the sweater she'd been looking for, just light enough for this weather, then got her car keys from the lamp table for the short drive to the market. Stepping out on the porch, she had to decide whether to take the sweater after all—it had gotten much warmer since she'd come home from school. She walked down the steps, carrying it, then saw with a rush of delight the first buds on her azalea bushes.

She went over and touched a couple of them, then instinctively leaned over to smell them, though they had no scent she could detect. As she straightened up she caught a glimpse of a newspaper almost completely hidden behind the bushes.

Today, again?

The paper lay in the small space between the back of the bushes and the front of the house. Furious—she couldn't believe she had to call them again!—she worked her way between the bushes, wondering how it could have gotten way back there. The paper lay in thick disarray on the dirt just below and to one side of the steps. It felt moldy as she began gathering it up. Then all at once she realized that it had probably blown down here from the steps. And that it wasn't today's paper. It was this past Sunday's.

TWENTY-TWO

DRIVING AWAY, Ben was aware of a sudden great release of tension, as though he were way back in time, running out of school, free of its pressures and of Old Cassaway in particular, into the clear air and all the cries of the schoolyard. She still—it was almost unbelievable—managed to grip him by the throat.

And it wasn't hard to picture himself back there again, in that grip, with no way out. And yet he'd been one of the good kids.

After just a block or two, though, he was thinking only of Nancy. It was so hard being only a few streets away from her and not at least calling. He pulled over to a phone but then sat there a while, trying to decide, and then as though on impulse went over to it.

He said only, "Nan," and there was a pause and she said, "Hold on," and now from another phone, "Where are you? I hear cars."

"Right around the corner. I just saw, you won't believe, Miss Cassaway."

"Oh gawd." It was as if there had never been any tension between them.

"See my hands? I still have the shakes."

She said, after a long moment, "Would you like to come over?"

"Love to."

"I have to go out for about an hour at the most, no one'll be here, but just come in and wait for me. I'll leave a key under one of the flower pots."

Back in the car, he sat looking out his open window without starting the motor. Though he was looking forward to seeing her, his head had become flooded again with Leopold. He'd never completely forgotten him but Leopold had been one of the vague memories of his life—a kid who showed up one day in the middle of the sixth grade and then was gone after starting the eighth, with no one missing him: one of those kids who seemed destined through no fault of their own to have a rough time in school. Now Cassaway had brought him back vividly.

But he had no idea, he really didn't, what exactly Cassaway had had against the kid—he wasn't even sure for a while if she'd treated him much differently from any of the others she used to lay into, like Jubb. But she had. With them it was just occasionally, though the threat was always there. And afterward they would use it as a kind of battle ribbon—Jubb swaggering down the hall, grinning, and even the girls who got it from her would laugh into their hands while their friends would joke with them. But Leopold crumbled early. And she'd never let him come out of it.

Ben remembered clearly when it started—maybe the second or third day they'd had her for English. She gave them a homework assignment that had something to do with poems they were going to read, and she tied it in with finding out where each kid's family originally came from to this country. The next day she called on everyone in turn, each one standing up to tell the class, then sitting down.

"Leopold?"

And as they did with everyone, all heads turned. Leopold rose, not a tall boy but gangly, his head slightly to the side on his thin neck.

"America," he said.

"America!" Her eyes widened. "We're all from America! I asked where your ancestors came from."

He grinned weakly—he had the kind of gums that were very red and looked angry. "America."

"Wipe off that grin. You hear me? Wipe that off!"

He began looking at the floor, his face crimson.

"Are you an Indian? Are you an American Indian?" The class, of course, was laughing by then.

He shook his head, seemed to want to say something but couldn't.

"Sit down, sit down!" And she waved him down and moved on, occasionally snapping a look at him.

After that, it seemed, he couldn't ever stand straight enough for her, talk fast enough, would always pronounce some word wrong...

Ben started the car.

He found himself thinking of the fistfight, and it made him cringe a little.

Cassaway had had to leave the room for a while and she asked Ben to be monitor. And Leopold had done something, maybe talked to someone, and when Cassaway came back Ben reported him. Later, leaving the building, he saw what looked like half the school waiting in the yard by the front steps, with Leopold in the middle and Jubb and Cookie and some of the others goading him into fighting.

Ben didn't want to fight the kid, knew he could easily beat him, and felt guilty about reporting him. But Leopold started dancing around him, jabbing the air, then moved forward and began hitting him, actually slapping at him like a girl, mostly missing or landing on Ben's arms. And though Ben began fighting, he would hit him only on the arms, the chest, never the face.

Still, it had ended with Leopold bleeding from the mouth—swinging, he had bitten his lower lip. And with everyone crowded around Ben and slapping him on the back and saying great things.

But that wouldn't have been anything to hold against him all these years, would it? It had been nothing compared to other fights Ben had had—Jubb included. Jubb had been one of those kids he'd never had any reason to talk to, but one day a grinning Jubb accidentally-on-purpose tripped him from behind and kept grinning until Ben's first swing. The fistfight eventually turned into a wrestling match, with Jubb on the bottom and unable to squirm out but refusing to say "I give up."

Ben was passing the Catholic church now, and a few blocks away the front of the elementary school. He glanced over at the rowhouses that faced it. He wasn't sure anymore which one Betsie had lived in, they all looked alike, but it could be the one with the large urn near the steps.

He thought of her thin face, with black bangs; pretty; thought of her, mostly just standing, head slightly bent and mouth open, next to her mother sitting on the stoop.

Leopold?

Was he the one? Or had Miss Cassaway done one more indignity to him across the years?

HE WAITED for Nancy on her porch, half-sitting on the railing.

He'd been trying—still was—to recall something he

might have known of Leopold. But he either couldn't remember or more likely never knew a single thing about him—what part of Barwyn he'd lived in, if he had any brothers or sisters, where he came from. And even—something Ben had simply assumed—if he'd really been as dumb as Cassaway made him out to be.

And then there was something else.

If Leopold had ever carried a murderous hatred from the school, surely it would be against Cassaway first of all. And all he would have to do to find her was wait outside the school.

Nancy pulled up shortly in her three-year-old Subaru, and she smiled at him as she got out. She was wearing a khaki skirt, a striped, boat-neck sweater and loafers. The cut of the sweater made her neck seem gracefully longer and, somehow, her red hair even shorter.

He came down and helped her with a mass of thick folders and papers she'd gone to pick up. He deposited them on one of the desks. She said, ''Been here long?''

''No. Just six or seven hours.''

''You didn't come in?''

''No, I was watching the yachts going by.''

She smiled, then said, ''It's gotten so warm.'' She went over to a window air conditioner and turned it on. It rattled a little before settling into a loud hum.

''Now I'm dying to hear,'' she said, sitting with him on the sofa. ''Tell me about Cassaway.''

''Well, for one thing I was at her house. In her house.''

''Her house?'' She looked amazed. ''Do you know I occasionally pass her on the street, I still never know when she's going to return my hello? And that doesn't make me all that exclusive.''

''I think she was just curious about what I wanted.''

''Did she remember you?''

''Oh, yes. Told me she'd always lived in fear of me.''

''Get serious.''

''Seriously, she said she remembered me. She called me Benjamin. I was only glad it wasn't Ben-jamin— she always used to call me Ben-jamin and it used to make my blood run cold. Anyway, all her pupils were wonderful then, nothing like today.''

''She said that?''

He nodded. ''The most they ever were was mischievous.''

''God, I don't know about yours but I remember her saying ours was the worst class she ever had—the worst.''

''Sounds familiar. Anyway, she only mentioned one kid—but look, let me go back a little.'' He told her about seeing Nevon, Shumlin and Cookie yesterday— and what Cookie had said about Jubb embezzling money, how the only kids Nevon said he hadn't liked in the class were Cookie and Jubb, and why it now seemed clear that the killer was after only certain people in the class. ''And here's something else that's interesting, very interesting. And very sad. Do you remember that girl, a retarded girl who lived across from the school? She was tied up in the woods, she escaped?''

Nancy was looking at him with a frown.

''There were all sorts of stories?'' Ben went on. ''There were stories she was raped, there were stories maybe nothing much really happened. Anyway, Nevon was the first one who mentioned her to me. He said she wasn't raped and they weren't even sure she was sexually molested, but she had mud all over her. He said Jubb and Cookie were the only ones he thought of in connection with it. And then I saw Cassaway and she names a kid, too. She said she even reported him to the police.'' He told Nancy about Leopold. ''You know she gave a lot of kids a rough time, but him she gave a rough, *rough* time. And I think it was only because he was—you know, different. One of those kids who look pathetic, always have a drippy nose, gums that are very red—they must have been infected now that I think of it.''

''We had a kid something like that. She was always on him.''

''This kid's name was Leopold Azza. You wouldn't happen to have known him, would you?''

''Leopold Azza?'' She thought, then shook her head.

''It's strange,'' Ben said, ''how that incident with Betsie came up twice. You remember her, don't you? A pretty girl. Almost always with her mother.''

''Of course I remember her. She was, you know, always around.''

Her face seemed in pain at the memory. He put his arm across her shoulders, but though she leaned against him her body was a little rigid. He rubbed her shoulder gently.

''I'm sorry,'' she said.

''About what?''

''I don't know,'' she said, shaking her head without looking up, ''but everything's death, everything's bad things these days. I don't want to think of death anymore, I don't want to think of bad things.''

TWENTY-THREE

BEN WOKE a couple of times during the night, very briefly and with a feeling of anxiety he was able to slip away from, back into sleep. When he finally woke in the morning it was there again, though it was fading now. And this time, from fragments of dreams he couldn't begin to put together, he knew it had something to do with Leopold.

Leopold...

Though trying hard he could barely remember him in Shumlin's class, other than that he'd entered it long after the sixth grade term began. Shumlin had been stern in his own way but Ben recalled it as so even-handed that he couldn't think of anyone who stood out as having received undeserved discipline or sarcasm. He couldn't even remember Leopold being given a hard time in the schoolyard then, though it must have happened—he'd been the kind of kid who attracted it. But it couldn't have been flagrant or he'd surely remember it.

He could remember it only when they moved on to Cassaway. It was as if, now that he was thinking about it, she'd made the kid an open city.

Ben-jamin.

Though she'd called Ben that, the kids never did.

Oh, maybe once or twice but he'd chased them around until they stopped.

But out in the yard the kids turned Leopold into Leo-*pold*.

"Leo-*pold!*" Cookie was the first one he remembered ever calling him that. He'd called it halfway across the yard, and it hadn't been for anything, just to call it. And Leopold, though he would stare dumbly at whoever was calling it, dumbly and maybe even with a little smile, never tried to stop it.

Then Ben thought of a couple of incidents in particular. Once, he and a bunch of the guys had been walking across a vacant lot after school when Leopold started running by. Someone grabbed his wool cap and everyone began tossing it around while Leopold ran in each direction and finally stood there in bewilderment.

"Leo-*pold!* Leo-*pold!*"

And though Ben had hated himself for it, he'd joined in, waving Leopold's cap at him until Leopold ran up to him, then tossed it to someone else. And while he'd never done anything else bad to him, except to report him that one time, he used to grin along with the rest of them when kids made fun of him. And he'd never tried to protect him, like that time Jubb, with Cookie and other kids grinning around him, kept pushing Leopold backward, accusing him of "telling on me to my mother."

Though Ben remembered wanting to jump in there and stop it—could even feel the anger of it now—he hadn't. And wouldn't have been caught dead even walking to or from school with him.

It was painful to remember. And to be sort of aware why.

That he hadn't wanted to be different, had felt different enough. Wanted only to be one of the guys.

BEN WISHED he could ask Shumlin for help, maybe he would know what happened to Leopold or would dig out his old address from the records. Yeah, good luck. Who else? Dan? Dan probably hadn't known anything more about Leopold than he himself did. And as Danny's mother used to say, whatever one of them knew, the other knew. Charleen DePolitto?

He tried her number. But after seven rings he put it down.

All he was doing, he knew, was trying to do something. But maybe an old neighbor of Leopold's would know if he was still in the city.

He tried to come up with someone else besides Charleen. He knew the names of most of the boys in the picture now, and all but a few of the girls, but still only knew where a handful lived. But what about Cookie?

Suddenly, thinking of Cookie, he automatically began thinking of him in connection with Jubb. Of that time Jubb had accused Leopold of going to "my mother"—it could mean Jubb and Leopold had lived close enough to know where each other lived or that their mothers were friends; something. And what Jubb knew, maybe his buddy Cookie knew, too.

It took about ten minutes for Cookie to come to the phone. He probably liked having people wait on the phone, too.

"Cookie, this is Ben Newman again. From school? I know you're busy, I hate to bother you—"

"Who?"

"Ben Newman? I was over to see you?"

"Oh. Yeah." Then Ben had to wait until he called something out to someone. When he came back: "Yeah."

"I know you're busy, Cook, but I was wondering if you might be able to help me on something. Do you remember a Leopold Azza from school? Maybe from Cassaway's class?"

It took a few moments before he said, "Oh. That geek."

"Do you have any idea what happened to him?"

"Christ, I don't know. How would I know?"

"Would you have any idea where he lived in Barwyn?"

"Christ, you want me to know the address? I don't know the address." All he knew was that Leopold had lived a couple of streets from where he himself lived as a kid. "He was adopted, you know. Well, he wasn't adopted," he corrected himself, "what do you call them? Foster. It was a foster home."

Leopold—even *that?* In a foster home?

Ben said, "Would you know the name of the people?"

"I used to, sort of—it was one of them kind of like Polish names or something. But I don't know. Wolanski? No. Look, I don't have time to think, I don't even have time to take a crap right now."

"Can I call you back later? I'd really appreciate it."

"Well," he said slowly, sourly, "do what you want. But don't appreciate it yet."

Sitting back from the phone, he kept thinking of Leopold in a foster home. On top of all his problems, that too. Moments later he was reaching over to answer the ringing phone.

"Ben, this is Ed Gowan."

Ben's face reflected his surprise. "Yeah. Hi."

"Look, I just want you to know you're an itch." But Gowan didn't say it unpleasantly. "I was out last night, I was having a nice time with the wife, and suddenly I'm thinking what if this guy's got something. You don't, I'm telling you you don't, but I want to hear it again. Got some time to come down here?"

ED GOWAN shook Ben's hand, holding an unlit cigarette in the other. And just the sight of it down by his side brought a sudden flashback of Gowan outside the Barwyn Theater, having tried to sneak in while smoking, and afterward smiling and slowly sucking down a butt between pinched fingers as the manager waited.

"I think I have these beat and then I don't," he apologized, lifting the cigarette. He wore, as usual, a button-down shirt and a neatly knotted tie, this time a paisley. Ben caught a glimpse of the small, holstered gun just to the rear of his right hip. "Look," Gowan said with a little smile, "my nightmare is this—that though you're all wrong you might turn out to be right—and I'm going to look like a horse's potato. So what say you go through it for me again, make sure I have it right."

Starting with Pat, Ben brought him up to the hit-and-run killing of Julia Neubauer on Saturday night; explained why he thought Pat's murder was a mistake and why he now felt that the deaths of George, Ellen and Julia were somehow linked to their having been in the same grammar school class. "And there's something you don't know," he went on, "that would have convinced me even if I wasn't before. I'm positive this son of a bitch is after me."

Gowan stared at him, frowning, as Ben told him

about his picture in the *Dispatch* and the phone call to his brother's house. Gowan, still frowning, said quietly, "Did you report this?"

"I am now."

"If you're so damn sure, why didn't you let someone know? Why didn't you call me, why'd you wait 'til I called you?"

Looking at him, Ben suddenly only wanted to get in a dig. "Well, I was getting a little tired of you people believing everything I was saying." Gowan smiled uncertainly. "And there's something else," Ben went on. "You happen to remember there was a retarded girl near the grammar school something happened to in the woods? Her name was Betsie? She broke away from whoever had her, her hands were tied?"

Gowan frowned. Then, slowly, "Yeah. I was a freshman in high school at the time. So?"

"Just that her name's been coming up." He told Gowan what Nevon had said about his immediate suspicion of Jubb and Cookie, and about Cassaway reporting Leopold to the police. "There were so many stories going around at the time, but Nevon says she definitely wasn't raped."

"That's what I heard, I remember my father saying it. Anyway *this,* I'm sure, is a bunch of crap. I remember my dad saying they thought it was kids at first but then they began looking for some guy—I know he had a record with kids. And when they finally caught up to him they found he'd killed himself."

Ben was about to ask him had he known Jubb and Cookie at school, when he recalled a scene near grammar school, on someone's front steps, where Jubb and Cookie and some other kid strained together to beat

Gowan in arm wrestling, only to sink exhausted to the ground after he put them down. So, instead he said, "You knew Jubb and Cookie."

"Sure. The Jubbs moved away years ago. But"— he shook his head—"I can't see him doing that. And Cookie—no way. He's all mouth but he wouldn't hurt a fly. And who's this other kid?"

Ben described Leopold for him, then went on about Jubb. "Cookie told me he thought Jubb has a record."

Gowan's face registered a touch of surprise. "I've seen Cookie a hundred times, he never mentioned it."

"Well, that's what he said. Leopold—I don't know, but if there was ever a kid who might have grown up in a rage—"

"And ended up making a million bucks," Gowan finished for him with a little smile.

"You're right, could be," Ben agreed. "The only reason I've even thought about Betsie is that she's been mentioned a couple times. But say we forget about her, say she has nothing to do with this. No one can tell me it's a coincidence that George, Ellen and Julia just happened to die violently within a short time of each other. And just happened to be in the same class."

"And there's you," Gowan said, looking at him.

"And there's me."

Gowan looked at him curiously. "What are you doing to protect yourself?"

"I try to be careful."

"I'd say that's a hell of a good idea. Now let me ask you something else. You say you think the same guy killed all four of them, your sister-in-law by mistake. Now if it turns out your sister-in-law was killed by''—he lifted a palm—''let's say someone else, there goes everything, right?''

''There was no 'someone else,' Ed,'' knowing of course he meant Harry.

Gowan kept looking at him. He started to put the still-unlit cigarette to his mouth but then lowered it. ''Look, being in Internal Affairs means you investigate cops. And I don't think I have to tell you, it doesn't make me Miss Congeniality in the department. But I'll pass it along.''

''Good enough.''

''Now, I want you to know I'm not taking back anything I told you before. I don't like the idea of you playing cop. In fact, I'm telling you not to. That's my official stance. But I'm not completely thick-headed— I know you're going to do whatever the hell you want. So what I'm saying, I'm going to do my damnedest to keep an open mind because in the end you just might make me the smartest guy in the department. But it also means you come to me if you come up with anything else, and I'll see what I can do. Okay?''

''Fine.''

''So what do you want to know?''

''Would you check to see if Jubb and Leopold have records?''

Gowan left him for about twenty minutes. When he came back, his face was hard. Jubb, that son of a bitch, did have a record. He'd received a suspended sentence in Pittsburgh for embezzlement, then served two years in Detroit for aggravated assault, and then got sent back there two years later for violation of parole. He'd been released and his whereabouts were unknown. Leopold Azza had no record. ''I'll see what I can do on Jubb,'' Gowan said. ''Another thing. If you give me the names of other kids in the class, I'll run a check on them."

"Great. I'll drop off what I've got."

Gowan walked with him part way down the corridor. "Let me say just one more thing," Gowan said.

Ben grinned. "You're going to ask me to forgive you—you really believe me now."

Gowan smiled thinly. "You yourself brought up the weakest point. Why just some of you? Why not Cookie, why not others in the class who've gotten a play in the papers? And there's that other party," he said.

Ben looked at him. "Miss Cassaway?"

Gowan nodded. "Sure. Miss Cassaway. I'd have loved to kill her myself."

BEN INTENDED GIVING Cookie at least a couple of hours before calling him again. But he held out only for an hour. A young voice, probably a teenager, answered.

"Yeah, Cookie's here," he said. "Who's this?"

"Tell him Ben Newman." Which could mean Cookie might never come to the phone.

After some five minutes the kid was back. "Cookie says to tell you he ain't sure, but it could be either of these."

And he gave him two names. Wonovski. Wolneki.

A quick look through the phone book showed no Wonovski's, but two Wolneki's. He didn't recognized either address as being in Barwyn, though they could be.

He tried to figure out what he would say if one of them turned out to be the right one. But he still wasn't sure as he lifted the phone. He got a busy signal twice at the first number before he tried the second.

A woman answered. She sounded too young to have been a foster parent back then.

Ben gave his name, then said, ''I hate to bother you but I'm trying to locate a fellow I went to school with back in the 'sixties, early 'seventies. And I wonder if you could help me. His name was Leopold…Leopold Azza?''

There was immediate silence, then, ''I'd better give you my father.''

He came on, gruffly. ''Leopold hasn't lived here in years. Who's this?''

Ben gave his name again. ''I'm trying to locate him and I hope you can help me.''

''Well, like I say he hasn't lived here in years.''

''Do you have any idea where he went after he left you?''

''Look, mister, I don't talk about things to strangers on the phone. Who are you anyway?''

''I'm a writer,'' Ben said. ''And there's something I want to discuss with him that could be important to him.''

''Well,'' the man said. And then: ''All right, come over, but just for a few minutes.''

TWENTY-FOUR

THE JOHN WOLNEKI HOME was in a section of Barwyn that seemed to have been grafted onto its outskirts rather than being an intrinsic part of it. It was an area of a few narrow, cobbled streets with wall-like stone rowhouses that gave it a look of an old mining town in Wales. Years ago there had been a textile mill here, and these had been the workers' homes.

A young woman holding a baby came to the door. Then she stepped aside and her father took her place. He looked to be in his sixties, had uncombed white hair and obvious dentures.

Ben said, "Hi, I'm Ben Newman. I appreciate your letting me stop over."

Wolneki looked at him carefully, then stepped back and kept looking at him as he came in. He didn't ask him to sit down. "You want to tell me what this is about?"

"I knew Leopold in grammar school—we were in the same class. But I never did know what happened to him after he left. And recently it's become very important that I find him."

"Important how?"

"Important to him." He had a crappy story prepared, about something he was writing of those years, but he was hoping his short answer would be good enough.

"You say you're a writer? For a newspaper?"

"No, I do magazine articles, books."

Wolneki didn't seem to know what to do, glanced over at his daughter. Then he said, slowly, "Well, the truth is I don't really know what's happened to him."

Then why in hell, Ben wondered, *did you agree to see me?* He said, "How long was he with you?"

"Only the time he went to Barwyn. He'd been in at least two other foster homes. He was a pretty bright kid," he added after a moment.

"I really knew very little about his personal life," Ben said. "All I know was I felt sorry for him."

"Hardly ever talked but he was a pretty bright kid. Real good at math. But I guess it didn't show at school, though I know he worked real hard. A strange sorta kid."

"Did he ever talk about what it was like for him at school?"

Wolneki thought, then shook his head. "Like I say, he didn't talk much."

"Do you have any idea where he went after he left here?"

He shook his head, then looked at his daughter again. There was, Ben sensed, an uneasiness about him now. "Just," Wolneki said, "that we turned him back to the woman."

"May I ask what woman?"

"You know, the one at the agency. The one we got him from. So we just gave him back." He paused; it was obvious something was disturbing him. "I guess it makes Rosa and me sound like real bad people but we weren't. Rosa, God rest her soul, Rosa and me didn't take him in just for the money. We needed the money but it wasn't just for the money.'' Even his look seemed to be trying to convince Ben. ''You want to know the truth why we gave him back? We got scared of him.''

Ben said nothing. Wolneki, he felt sure, would go on. This might even be why he'd had him come over; wanted to talk out whatever was troubling him.

''We got scared of him,'' he repeated. ''Something happened—I don't know exactly what; to this day I don't—but something happened to a little girl around here. In the woods. Someone tied her up. You were here, you say. Do you happen to remember that?''

''Yes.''

''The police—they had this idea he did it. I don't know why. They kept asking us where he'd been, what time, you know. And they must have questioned him two, three times. But then one of the lawyers from the agency did something, I don't know what, made them stop.''

''Did you think he did it?''

''I don't know what to say. No, I didn't, but then, you know, we wondered. He kept saying he didn't. But what scared us was Rosa found herself pregnant with our first, Kathy here's sister, and there was no way we were going to keep him, we were too scared.''

Ben asked him what agency they'd gotten him from. Wolneki smiled vaguely, ''One downtown. The lady—this lady we got him through, I know she retired a number of years ago.''

''Would you happen to know where she is?''

Wolneki looked at him. ''I know where she is.'' He said it almost in a monotone, as if he were thinking something out. ''We got another youngster from her

after Kathy was born, so we knew her real well."
Then, frowning, "But I don't feel free to give out her
name, if that's what you want."

"Well, could I ask you to try to get in touch with
her and give her my phone number?"

He frowned. "Well, I guess."

Ben marked it down on a piece of paper Wolneki
gave him.

"If you can't reach her," he said, "would you call
me?"

Wolneki nodded, then took a couple of steps toward
the door. Ben, following him, asked, "Did you know
anything about Leopold's family?"

Wolneki shook his head. "And I wouldn't know
who does. He was one of those cases they find a baby
on the sidewalk or somewhere. I don't know for sure
where he got that name, but I heard one of the nurses
gave him her grandfather's."

It wasn't until Ben was in his car that, an emptiness
in his gut, he thought of Leopold standing by his desk
with that embarrassed, red-gum smile, insisting on
America as his total heritage to Cassaway.

What the hell else could the poor little son of a bitch
say?

IN HIS APARTMENT, he got out the class picture and
began writing down names for Gowan. He paused after a few moments, to concentrate on the faces again.

Cookie, Jubb, and that kid there, Ron Jansen, second from the left, and even that girl there, Dora, next
to Ellen, they were kids it had been easy to dislike.
To hate. But Ellen? George? Mouse-like Julia? Real
good kids. What could they have done back then to
have brought on this horror after all these years? And

him? All he could remember of himself in class, every class, not just Cassaway's, was this quiet kid who obeyed every instruction, brought his homework in on time, never cheated, was quick to volunteer for tasks; *wanted* them. And his hand would always be shooting up to answer questions, and in Cassaway's class he would try to keep his eyes on her as if, even though he was scared shitless of her half the time, he really wanted her to pick the three-by-five card with his name.

Even Cassaway, looking at the class picture, had pointed to George and Ellen and Julia and called them "nice."

Of course, she'd begun thinking of almost all her long-ago pupils as nice, but she'd had every reason to with Ellen. Always used to call on her to read her homework, her compositions. And Julia—so quiet, it made him seem noisy in comparison. And that left-handed writing of hers, so elegant that Cassaway and at least one other teacher he couldn't remember, would have her demonstrate it on the blackboard. He could remember a few times that Cassaway even had Julia walk up and down the aisles, showing her work to kids on either side.

And he and George…Cassaway was always calling on them for her "jobs," opening and closing of the windows, bringing in stacks of books from the closet out in the hall, or opening and closing the folding doors between classrooms for assembly, or— He stopped, with a frown.

No, it couldn't be that.

That?

That the four of them had been among her favorites?

And was that why it didn't matter what they were today—it was what they'd been *then?*

Quickly he looked at the picture again. Which other kids? He was sure Cassaway had pointed specifically to at least one more. But who? He kept looking. Yes, Alan Green, who'd lived next door to her—that was why, the kids used to say, that even though he was pretty dumb she not only never raised her voice at him but never even gave him one of those looks.

He took out the phone book, found a listing for an Alan Green.

He put his hand on the phone, trying to decide what to do. If nothing else, just to find out if it was the same Green, that he was alive. He lifted the receiver, began to make the call.

After nine or ten rings he slowly put it down.

JOHN WOLNEKI CALLED soon afterward. He'd reached the woman, Mrs. Brenner, and she'd called him back after getting in touch with the agency.

"I didn't know any of this," he said, "but she told me they couldn't get any more foster couples to keep him very long and then he disappeared. But that's not all. When she just called the agency she learned that he's dead. Died about two years ago."

TWENTY-FIVE

HE WAS AWARE, as he hung up, of a gnawing sense of disappointment. Leopold behind all this made sense; everything fit. In fact, it was only now that he could see how he'd been putting himself back there in Leopold's shoes, hating the kids, hating her most of all.

Hating her most of all, for she had triggered the abuse and fed it.

And now with Leopold out of it, it seemed that all that was left to him was the hate.

JOANNIE CALLED that evening. She said hesitantly, "I just wondered if you're, you know, maybe if you'd like to come over."

"Tell me what's happening."

"I don't know. Daddy's upstairs." He pictured her struggling against tears.

"Where's your grandmother?"

"She had to go home for a while. My grandpop is sick, he needs her."

"Honey, I'll be right over." He felt so goddamn sorry for her, so sorry.

Walking to his car he did, automatically, what he'd been doing the past few days: looked around carefully, then after driving off the parking lot he made quick turns onto several side streets before settling back, though with an occasional glance in the rearview mirror. And yet turning into Harry's street, his headlights opening the darkness, he realized that for a little while he had stopped thinking of any danger. Realized it now that he was back at the only address that voice on the phone apparently had for him.

But even here, as he parked behind Harry's car in the lighted driveway, any menace seemed unreal. Maybe it was because everything looked so normal— lights on in all the houses, a group of teenagers standing under a streetlight near a car on the next driveway, a man waiting on the sidewalk for a basset hound to shuffle toward him.

Joannie came to the door, gave him a tight hug, her cheek against his chest. "My hippie uncle," she said, still squeezing him.

"Me?"

"Yes, you."

"Honey, I'm as square as they come."

"You are not. How many kids have uncles who write books and articles and get people out of jail?"

"The institutions are filled with them." He kissed her on the forehead. "Tell me about your dad."

"You know," and she shrugged. "He's still upstairs."

As he walked to the stairs she called after him, "I hope you didn't eat."

"Me? When I hear you've got beef jerky?"

She laughed. "Next time. Will pizza be okay?"

"Fine." He called upstairs, "Harry?" When he didn't get an answer: "Har?"

"I'm up here," Harry said quietly.

The door to his study was partly open. Harry was

sitting leaning back at his desk, arms folded. He looked at Ben with a slight frown. "Close the door, will you?"

Ben closed it, looking at him. "What's the heavy thinking?"

"I don't know. Nothing." But he said it strangely. He was staring at the far wall, the shelves that lined it and the other walls filled mostly with medical books, interspersed with many of the porcelain figures he and Pat had collected on their trips and at antique shops. Then he looked at Ben. "I just called my service. One of the detectives called. Wants me to call him."

Ben felt his pulses quicken. "Which one?"

Harry's face began to show a tightening of anger. "That guy from Homicide. Lafferty."

The fellow, Ben thought, McGlynn was supposed to talk to for him. "Did you tell your lawyer?"

"Christ, I just heard." There was real anger in it now, and the question hadn't deserved any.

"I'd do it first thing," Ben said.

"I don't know. I'll see."

Ben could just see him going into one of those mule stances he remembered so well as a kid. And you could never talk him out of it—his parents probably because they rarely tried, and Ben simply because he never could.

But though Ben wanted to back off, words came out: "Harry, whatever you do, don't call the guy back. First talk to your lawyer."

"I don't know." Each word had a snap to it. He was fingering a letter opener, staring down at it. His ears were fiery.

"Harry," Ben said. Just that. But Harry still didn't

look up. "Harry, I just want to say this. You've got a lawyer. Talk to him, listen to him."

Harry's eyes suddenly flared as he looked at him. He slapped the letter opener on the desk. "I told you, I'm sick of it! Sick of lawyers! My lawyer isn't me."

"Harry, let me ask you something." Ben leaned toward him. He didn't want to say anything more but he couldn't stop himself. "What do you think this cop's going to say to you? That you're a great guy? Fine. But let him tell it to your lawyer. Harry, you're just looking for a lot more trouble. Use your head."

"I'll see."

"What do you mean you'll 'see'?"

"What I said. I'll see. I'll see."

Ben stared at him, his frustration, anger, mounting. He straightened up. And then he couldn't help it, it just came out: "Then go ahead! Go see!"

Harry looked at him, startled. "What're you raising your voice for?"

"Harry, don't give me anything about raising my voice, okay? I don't want to hear that! Do whatever you want. Whatever you want!"

"Just keep it down," Harry said, gesturing. He looked away.

Ben tried to control the sudden heaving of his chest. He wanted to punch him, turn his face around and just, just... Harry had always had this ability, going back forever, to end things on his own terms. No wonder it was easier to just stay away.

"The pizza will be here in five minutes," Joannie called from downstairs.

Ben went downstairs. All he wanted to do now, though he would eat with them and talk of other things, was run the hell away from here.

"HARRIS," HIS BOSS SAID, "I'm tellin' you, I'll pay you double overtime."

"Can't." He was out of breath; he'd just carried in the last of the three sets he hadn't been able to fix at customers' houses.

"But it's an emergency. I promised they'd have it first thing in the morning. You see I got no one else. Double."

"I can't." Harris glared at his boss, then made sure he'd turned in all the checks and cash, and now was walking quickly to the door and over to his car.

He didn't care if it meant his job. All he'd been able to think about all day, and maybe it was even why he couldn't fix the three sets, was going to the brother's house again, this time up to the door, this time with the gun.

Tell me! Tell me where he is!

He could see himself screaming it.

He was barely aware as he drove that it was dusk now and darkening fast with low-hanging clouds, until he realized that oncoming cars had their lights on and that his were still off. How could he be so dumb to drive without lights and with a gun in the glove compartment?

The street, the goddamn doctor's street now, two blocks from the house. He slowed up, constantly glancing over to his right as though somehow he would miss it after all this time. He came to an intersection—Newman's was two houses from the opposite corner—and crossed it at a crawl. And then, at the house, in the middle of the street, his foot suddenly went hard on the brake.

Two cars!

The past few nights there'd only been the one.

He tried to make out the license numbers from here, but couldn't for some reason though the driveway was floodlighted and the downstairs lights were on. He pulled to the curb. He kept staring over, then all around; no one, as far as he could see, was outside. He shouldn't do this, he warned himself, he shouldn't take the chance.

But it was as though something burst in him, and he got out and walked closer to the driveway.

He felt so exposed, so naked.

Just a little closer. Only a little.

And then, on the car nearest to him...738.

His numbers!

He backed away slowly, then tried not to run to his car.

He drove off quickly, close to panic that someone had spotted him. He drove around the block and found a spot across the intersection, where he parked among a scattering of other cars. Here he had a good view of the driveway as well as a little of the house. Sitting in the grayness between two lampposts, he kept telling himself not to look at the clock on the dash, time would only go slower. But he kept looking.

Lucky! How he'd hoped he wouldn't have to go up to that house and do something that could have been so stupid.

He opened the glove compartment and glanced in, though it was the second time since leaving the shop that he'd checked to see if the gun was there.

He didn't even want to use it. He hadn't done all this, come so far, just to do something obvious. But how else beside the gun?

A bridge, he was thinking, where was there a bridge, say, on a quiet road? Or where was a cliff?

It was after ten when he thought, wasn't sure, that he saw another light go on in the house. Then was sure: it was the light from the foyer as the front door opened. And now he saw the car's rear lights go on as it backed out.

It was heading in his direction. As it neared the corner, signaling a left, he started the motor. He got to the corner a few moments after it turned. He raced to catch up, then slowed up and stayed back—maybe a little too far back, another car might pull in.

Ahead, a traffic light turned yellow; the other car went through. It turned red an instant before he got there, but he kept going, almost afraid to look, but looking, in the rearview mirror for the sudden fireworks of police lights. By the time he looked ahead the other car was making a turn into another street. He followed, but a car pulled between them before he could get closer.

He kept inching out and back, not so much to try to pass—too many cars were coming in the other direction—but to make sure it was still there. Then he saw it peel off onto another street.

As he made the turn the car was disappearing into the parking lot of some apartment building. He raced there but was too late to see where it had gone—it had probably slipped into a spot, in the middle of what looked like a million cars. He drove through the lot but couldn't see any headlights going off or anyone walking. He found a space toward the back, near a sign that said Visitors.

He got out and walked cautiously to the entrance of the building, but he could see a security guard sitting at the desk in the small outer lobby. He turned quickly and started to head back.

He didn't know if the guy saw him, if he was suspicious why he'd suddenly walked away. For a few moments he felt almost dizzy, couldn't remember where on the lot he'd parked his car. Then he saw a public phone against one of the far walls.

He wasn't sure if he had enough change, but he did. He got Information, asked if she had anything for a Benjamin Newman in the Sylman Apartments.

"I'm sorry, sir," she answered shortly, "but it's a private listing."

But you stupid bitch, you just gave it to me.

But which apartment?

Hanging up, he took several deep breaths. In his mind he was somehow finding his way to Newman's floor, to Newman's door, and now he was tapping on it lightly and Newman was opening it, and his face was suddenly terrified, he was falling back—

But he had to calm down, he had to. Now of all times he mustn't, mustn't, mustn't make a mistake. And he must always remember that Benjamin Newman—no, Ben-jamin Newman—wasn't the last one.

TWENTY-SIX

THE FOLLOWING DAY Ben was stopped by the ringing of the phone as he was about to leave for Gowan's office. He stood near the door as the message came over his answering machine.

"Ben," his editor said, "this is Carter. Call me, please."

Ben hesitated—he was anxious to get to Gowan's with the names of these kids. He made the call to the editor, standing up.

"Ben, how you doing?"

"Good, Carter. You?"

"Real good. I know you're busy as hell but I'm wondering about the Dougherty case, where we stand."

Ben raised his eyes to the ceiling, remembering that he should have called Carter to let him know when he'd have the story. Dougherty, in his early twenties, had been shot dead in suburban Havertown and his handful of dollars taken by two thugs as he was making a delivery of a couple of cheesesteaks. They had been found guilty a few days ago and were awaiting sentencing.

"Sorry I didn't call," he apologized, "but I'll have it for you about the middle of next week."

"Good enough. I'm thinking of using it for *All-Clue,* though I also have a spot open in *Pursuit.*"

"You'll have it." And he would, somehow, though Ben hadn't set up an interview yet. But he had a good source there.

They talked on, about which of Carter's magazines could use what, and as they did Ben could picture him putting a glowing butt to the cigarette in his mouth without losing a word, and always maintaining a certain distinguished air.

"Okay, Ben. We'll be in touch. You take care."

"You too."

As he put down the phone, he thought of how Carter missed little: was forever keeping up to date on crimes and the status of crimes through news services, newspapers and contact with contributors. But it wasn't until he was at the elevators that he thought, with a sickening feeling, of Carter one day calling and saying: *How they doing with the murder of that doctor's wife?*

GOWAN WASN'T IN and no one knew when he'd be back, but as Ben was walking down the hall he saw him coming in his direction with another man.

Gowan said, frowning slightly, "We didn't have an appointment, did we?"

"No, I just dropped off the list you wanted. Would you happen to have a few minutes though?"

"Can't right now, got a meeting. But call me in a couple hours."

Ben watched them walk off. One of the things he wanted to tell him was about Leopold's death, but most important about Cassaway's "favorites," and how that could include at least one other kid—her former neighbor Alan Green.

And about no answer—still—at Green's place.

Ben had tried again last night and then this morning.

Walking out of the building he went to a phone. Again no answer there. But Information gave him Green's address.

A half hour later he was parked on a narrow, tree-bordered residential street downtown, in front of a "Father, Son and Holy Ghost" house—one of a row of expensive little stone and brick rowhouses, with basically one room on each of their three floors. He rang the bell without expecting an answer, and didn't get one at the house to the right, either. But a young woman with long blond hair and a plaid shirt over-hanging her jeans answered the door on the left.

"No, I don't know where Mr. Green is—I haven't seen him for at least two weeks. But that isn't un-usual."

Ben said, "I'm not sure if I have the right one. Would you happen to know if he ever lived in Bar-wyn?"

"No, I don't. You'd think," she said, "people live this close they'd see each other all the time, know each other pretty well. But it's basically hello, how are you, if that. I don't know anyone in his family. All I really know is that he's single and works out of his house as a freelance commercial artist."

Back in the car Ben kept looking at the house. He remembered Alan with a round face, who used to do particularly well in woodshop. It wasn't hard picturing him as an artist.

He found a blank, letter-sized envelope in his glove compartment, removed some receipts it held and wrote Green a note, giving his address and phone number. Then he went to put it through the slot near the bottom of the door. But as he opened the lid he could see it was almost completely blocked on the other side with mail. He squeezed the envelope through, then straightened up, no longer just uneasy about him.

GOWAN STILL WASN'T IN when Ben called him from his apartment. No, the lieutenant hadn't said when he'd be back. "Please have him call Ben Newman. It's important."

Important? It could be urgent. Or nothing at all. A different Alan Green. Or the same one away on a trip who'd forgotten to stop his mail.

He thought of calling Cassaway. After all, she'd lived next door to the Greens, might have kept in touch, might be able to give a name or number to call. But it was too early for her to have come home from school.

Too early, but he tried on the chance she hadn't gone in for some reason—Cassaway whom he couldn't remember ever missing a day.

He held on even after he was sure there would be no answer, but his mind was turning to Nancy. He'd been thinking of her off and on all day, had been waiting for some vague kind of right time to call—not about any of this, he wouldn't lay this heaviness on her anymore, but just to say hello, see how she was.

One of her employees answered.

"Is Nancy there, please?"

"May I tell her who's calling?"

It was a couple of minutes before she came on, away from the clacking and other background noises.

"Nancy. Me. How are you?"

"Okay." But her voice sounded strained. "And you?"

"All right. Nan, I just wanted to say hello, see how you are."

"I'm all right. I'm—it's just that I'm terribly busy right now. Over my head, really."

"Well, what say I call you some other time?"

"I'm really sorry about right now."

"That's okay. You take care. I'll call you again."

He waited for her to hang up, which he sensed more than anything, and then he set down the phone, silently.

GOWAN CALLED a half hour later. Ben, forcing his thoughts away from Nancy, filled him in quickly, adding that the only thing that still didn't fit was that someone would be out to kill Cassaway's "pets" and not touch her.

"That's a pretty damn big only," Gowan said.

"Or for some reason he's just not gotten around to her yet. Ed, would you check to see if there's a missing persons on Alan Green? And Miss Cassaway, would you ask her if she knows where any of the Greens live? And maybe find out if anything unusual had been happening to her lately—like getting strange phone calls?"

"Just on the little you're telling me?" Gowan retorted. "No way. All I'd be doing is scaring the crap out of her."

"Or maybe doing her a big favor."

"Come on." Gowan's voice had a sharp edge to it now. "Get off it. I'm not scaring the shit out of her for no damn reason."

"Well, you do what you want. I've told you what I'm afraid of and now you know everything I know, and you do what you want."

"Look." Gowan's voice was rising. "I've been going along with you. But now you're being a wise-guy."

"I'm sorry I sound like a wise-guy, I don't mean to." But it was hard to even sound calm when all he wanted to do was hang up on him. "I only asked would you want to see her or call her. You don't want to, fine. I'm not telling you what to do."

"You could fool the hell out of me."

"Hold on, hold it." And now he couldn't keep himself back. "Didn't you say it was okay for me to come to you? You'd help? Was I hearing things? Well, let me tell you this: I told you what I was afraid of, okay? But you don't want to talk to Cassaway? Fine. But now it's on you. Okay? Whatever happens is on you!"

"Good."

But a couple of hours later Gowan called back, just as friendly as if nothing had happened between them. He sounded a little troubled, though—about Jubb, it turned out.

"I talked to Jubb's old man. Claims he hasn't seen him in years, doesn't want to see him. That guy, I don't know," as if he'd heard something that was strictly police business, something he had to think about. But his voice brightened when he spoke about Miss Cassaway. "I'm home now, I had to be in Barwyn anyway, so I just saw the lady. Christ, Cassaway. The only thing bothering her is that once in awhile someone, she doesn't know who, delivers her a paper she doesn't want."

STARING OUT AT the gray, drizzly early evening, Ben kept going back to why the kids and not Cassaway.

He tried to place himself back in that class again,

to see it, feel it. Strange, how he couldn't remember anything of her class but the fear. Not a book report, not a composition, not a bit of grammar, not a poem she'd had them read, not a moment of free laughter, just the little laugh she'd let you have when one of her own rare smiles permitted you to release it. Nothing, nothing but the fear, and always trying to stay on her good side. For you really never knew.

Like that time, one of several times actually, when he'd thought she was going to explode on him.

She'd been standing in front of the class, going through compositions she was about to hand back, when suddenly she grabbed up a couple of them and strode down his aisle. He was sure she was coming right at him, but then stopped as though confused and went around to another aisle and ordered Leopold to stand up.

"This handwriting, this handwriting!"—and then she held up another composition, Julia's—"This is what I expect! I'm not standing for this! Who do you think you are? What kind of school do you think this is?" And on and on, with Leopold standing there, occasionally sniffling, unable to stop even with her "Stop that! Don't you even have a *tissue?*"

And afterward Leopold sitting down and glowering from down near his chest at everyone staring at him.

It seemed, as Ben remembered it, that she'd let them all stare at him a while.

His own stare, he knew, had been more out of relief than anything else, though he'd squirmed inwardly for him. But what good was the squirming, when he'd stared?

No wonder Leopold would hate him. And her. And

all of them, not just her favorites, but especially her favorites.

Could see him wanting revenge, managing to hold it in all these years, but then it building, growing.

Ben stopped all at once, sharply aware he'd been thinking of Leopold alive. As the only one it could be. The only one he could understand it being.

But he'd died about two years ago, the agency said. Leopold would have been, what, about twenty-eight? Twenty-nine?

Ben was sure the agency was right; what were the odds against that kind of mistake?

But suddenly he was curious; hadn't thought of this before.

How—why?—would the foster care agency know of his death years later as an adult?

JOHN WOLNEKI didn't question why Ben wanted to talk to the woman from the agency, Mrs. Brenner. "No, I don't mind calling her. I'll give her your message."

Some twenty minutes later Ben's phone rang. It was Mrs. Brenner, a woman whose voice was a little crackly with age.

"I understand that you want to talk to me about Leopold Azza," she said.

"Yes," he said. "And I really appreciate your calling."

"Well, I don't know what else I can say. It's all been a long while ago."

Ben said, "I just want to ask you something. From what I understand, you apparently didn't know Leopold died until you called the agency."

"That's right."

"I'm curious about something. Did they happen to tell you how they knew?"

"Yes, and it's sort of strange. Someone, let's see if I get this straight, someone called there about two years ago and asked for me, but I was long retired by then. He said he was a friend of Leopold's, that Leopold had always spoken highly of me and in fact all the people at the agency, and he thought we'd want to know that he'd died. In a car accident. I didn't know about this before because I just got back from living in Florida. My husband died, you see, and I wanted to live near my daughter. And I had no reason to call the agency anymore."

"Do you know if the fellow who called said where it happened?"

"Somewhere in Ohio. Mrs. Clemens—she's the one who took the call but she couldn't remember where."

"Did she say if he gave his name?"

"I asked her that, and she was pretty sure he did but she couldn't remember it."

LONG MOMENTS AFTER he hung up Ben just sat there, mind racing.

No matter how many ways he looked at it, that story didn't make all that much sense.

Leopold, after failing to be placed by the agency, drops out of sight. Years later he dies and a friend of his, knowing how much he'd thought of Mrs. Brenner, of the whole agency, calls to tell them of his death. But why if Leopold had this feeling for her, for the others, hadn't he ever called there over the years?

It could be true. A guy silently cherishing the memory of people who had tried to help him. But who was it who'd called?

Was it someone, perhaps, Leopold had told his life story to, who knew all the names of the people who'd hurt him—and was filled now with all his hatred? Or—and this was the thing that kept nipping at him—could it actually have been Leopold himself? To be able to kill and yet be dead? The same kind of mind that could make George Havers' murder a suicide, Ellen's an accident, Julia's a hit-and-run?

His hand reached out at the sudden ringing of the phone.

"Ben," Nancy said in a quiet voice.

"Nan." He had to take a long breath. "I'm glad you called."

"Ben, I'd like to see you. Can I see you?"

And from the sudden tremor in her voice, he knew something was wrong.

TWENTY-SEVEN

DOWN IN THE parking lot in the rain, a car moved slowly between the rows of cars, then quickly swung into a space, maneuvering back and forth until it settled in. The driver pulled up the handbrake fiercely, then sagged a little. After all his bad luck today it was hard to believe this.

He'd lost Newman in the traffic this morning and had come back here three times without finding the car. And now there it was, in that row way in front of him. He turned on the motor shortly, just to work the wipers, then turned it off. The rain seemed to be slowing up. He stared at the car through the gathering and sliding drops. He kept drawing in sharp little breaths.

Just—a little kid!

God, all he'd been was a little kid! And a *good* kid, a real good kid!

Like, how he'd always sit with his hands folded as hard as he could on his desk, shoulders straight, back stiff, but still always being blamed for something. And on top of it, it was always, "Ben-jamin, you go out for the books and pass them out," or "George, take this to the principal's office," or Ellen this and Julia that, and Alan, Alan who couldn't do anything wrong. And their turning their heads, with those little smiles and *looks,* when she'd make him stand up, like that time she'd held up the paper he had worked three hours on—"This handwriting, you think you can get away with this? Not here, mister, not here!" Three *hours.* "Here's how it's done—thank you, Julia." And "Thank you, Ben-jamin," for reporting him that time when all he'd done when she was out of the room was try to make the class laugh. And that girl, that Betsie…

He straightened up quickly, seeing a figure come out of the building. But it was a false alarm—a woman, followed by another woman.

He had to fight the pull just to stand outside the car.

He didn't know how he was going to do it, but however, whatever, it was him next, no matter how long he had to wait here. Him next and then her.

Yeah. Cass-a-way.

AT FIRST, stepping outside, Ben thought it had stopped raining. But now he could see the drizzle against the lights outside the marquee, could feel the little stings as, swinging on his raincoat, he walked into the parking lot. He didn't button it in his hurry to get to his car, and to her.

Cars were coming in and out. Several women were emerging from the car next to his, a couple of them opening umbrellas and waiting for the others.

He put on the wipers as soon as he started the motor, and backed out of the spot without warming it up. A mistake, he realized instantly, when it stalled. It stalled again at the exit from the lot and he had to rev the motor awhile before entering the street. Then it threatened to stall again at a red light, but he kept revving it, then it was running smoothly.

His rearview and side-view mirrors sparkled with

headlights. He adjusted the rearview mirror to dim them to dull white coins in the darkness as he maneuvered through several turns.

It was as he was nearing Barwyn that he noticed a car trying to pass the car directly behind him—its lights kept pulling out, then drawing back. He looked away, then happened to glance at the side-view mirror just as the second car curved in behind him. He expected it to try to pass him at some point, but it didn't, even though there was almost no traffic coming the other way.

For some reason he didn't think anything of it until he made a turn that would lead into Barwyn. And the lights behind him turned, too. He kept looking at them, alarmed. He sped up, then in a little while slowed down. The lights neither diminished nor grew; just kept pace.

He turned again, onto a street where he had to turn, and the lights floated with him. His pulses quick, he kept shooting glances in the mirrors. He would try another turn, a turn he didn't have to make, and he let one intersection go, then another, then made a fast left at the third. But suddenly there were so many lights in his mirrors, it was such a busy street, that he couldn't tell whether the other car had followed.

He made another turn, and again his mirrors were filled with sunbursts.

After a few moments he pulled sharply to the curb, turning off the lights and clicking the doors locked. A number of cars went by. Including, he wondered, *that* one? Or somewhere back there was it against the curb, too?

Or had he been imagining it? He could have imagined it.

He kept looking back, then swung out with his lights still off, not turning them on until he made a quick right. But then he had to stop fast: a truck was parked with flashing lights halfway in the street, and by the time he pulled around it there were lights again in his mirrors.

He made several more turns, sometimes with just blackness behind him, other times lights—and suddenly he was aware that he'd stopped simply fleeing, that a part of him was looking, was trying to find out for sure if someone was really following him. He was aware, too, that when he thought of someone behind him, it was Leopold—Leopold older, but with the same face, even the snot, wanting all Cassaway's favorites dead and perhaps saving her for last, the best for last; maybe even to be able to say to her: *See?*

He knew he was somewhere in Barwyn but for several moments he wasn't sure where. But it began straightening itself out as he drove, then finally jelled into a familiar area when he saw a supermarket ahead, the Acme a few blocks from Nancy's house.

What he mustn't do was drive to Nancy's.

Surely, even if someone had been following him, he'd lost him. Still, he mustn't drive there, lead him there.

He turned into the supermarket lot. It was crowded and brightly lighted. There was a phone near the entrance and he parked as close to it as he could, in a line of cars. It had stopped drizzling and people were casually walking in and out of the store, others unloading their carts by the open trunks of their cars. Inserting coins, he almost dropped some in his hurry.

"Nancy," he said.

"Ben, where are you?"

He told her. "Look, I don't know, I really can't be sure, but I think I've been followed from my apartment."

"What do you mean, followed?"

"I mean followed in the car. Like I say, I don't know for sure. But even if I was—"

"He knows you? He's after you?"

"Nancy, even if I was followed I'm sure I lost him. But again I don't know, I can't be sure. But I want you out of this. I won't be over."

"Ben."

"Tomorrow. I want to see you, God knows. But I'll check into someplace else and—"

"I want to see you, I'm coming right over."

"Nancy! No!"

"I'll be there, I'll be right over."

"I'm telling you no! Now listen—"

"I'll be there." And she hung up.

He waited for her, angry and worried, by the phone, under the store's overhang. He didn't see her pull into the lot or park her car; she was just suddenly walking quickly from one of the rows behind his car. She had on a light blue raincoat that hung open. And, something he'd never seen on her before, she was wearing large glasses, with thin, horn-rimmed frames.

"Ben, how do you know? Tell me." Her face was etched with fear.

"Christ, you shouldn't— You should have listened!" Then, "Let's go over here."

They stood off by themselves, away from the doors.

"Please tell me."

"Nancy, look," since he still couldn't seem to convince her of the urgency, "I know this guy's looking for me. I think but I can't swear he was following me just now, but I do know he's looking for me. That I know. Now go home."

She was staring at him, her eyes wide. "But what about you? What are you going to do?"

"I said I'll check in somewhere. Now I want you to go. I'll call you."

She kept staring at him. Then, in a strained way, "But tonight you really don't know if you were followed."

"Nancy, I've told you."

She kept looking at him in anguish. Then she reached out her hand and took his and put her fingers between his fingers. She squeezed hard, then he squeezed back, though not hard: the bones seemed fragile. "I want to be with you," she said. "Even if it's just to sit in the car."

"Nan."

"Please?"

They went over to his car. Although he was parked under a light she came up close against him, her face on his chest. He put his arms around her and brought her in tighter. He was still churning from the ride but it was easing away now. She kept rubbing his arms, but when he tried to raise her face for a kiss she kept it down.

They held each other silently for a while.

"You know," he said, looking down at her, "I haven't kissed you yet with glasses."

"Yes, you have," she said without looking at him.

"No," catching on. "Contacts. Well, I mean real glasses."

This time she let him lift her face, and he kissed her lightly on the lips, then fully. But now her face was against his cheek.

"Oh, Ben." It had such a sad sound to it that he stared down at her. "Take me somewhere," she said. "Just ride."

She moved away from him and sat with her head back, staring ahead. He looked at her, then started the motor and was moving before he remembered that he didn't want to take her anywhere in *his* car. He drove along the supermarket curb. He wanted to turn back and take her car, but he was close to the exit now and it suddenly seemed foolish. He drove out to the street. She put her head against his shoulder.

"Ben," she said after several moments, "I want to talk to you." He started to look at her but she said, "No. Just let me talk. And don't look at me."

He looked ahead. But a minute or so went by and she'd said nothing; seemed to be pressed harder against him. He drew to the curb and started to turn to her, to put his arm around her, when a glance in the mirror stiffened his body. Headlights had just died behind him, near the intersection. At the same curb. He kept looking at the mirror. She sensed it and sat up. "What is it?"

He shook his head slowly. "I don't know. Probably nothing."

But he kept looking at the mirror. He could see nothing in the darkness. Still looking at the mirror, he began to pull out slowly, a gradual test. But the lights didn't go on back there; he could see no sign of the car moving. He was halfway into the street now. And this time when he looked over his shoulder he could see the car, its headlights off, drawing away from the curb.

He turned at the next corner, at a moderate speed, not wanting to panic her, wanting to be positive—

though he was positive, it had to be. And now the other car was turning this corner, headlights suddenly on and as though clearing the way as it turned, and fixing themselves like spotlights in his mirrors. His foot went hard on the gas now, and barely eased up through another turn, and then went hard on it again.

"Ben!" Nancy swung around, facing him.

Staring straight ahead, trying to keep his voice steady: "Get ready! If I can, I'll stop. Just seconds. And out—get out! Run!"

"No!" She was shaking her head wildly.

"I'll stop! At a house! Somewhere!"

"No! Don't slow up! He'll—" Her face was close to his.

He made another turn. The headlights followed. Still another turn. Still following. A red light ahead, and he pressed hard on the horn and sped through. The other car was racing through, too. He kept blowing the horn, then needed both hands on the wheel, was going to make another turn. He turned, tires screeching. A car, two cars were coming this way. He raced by them; the lights stayed close.

He kept shooting wild glances to each side.

Stop—maybe stop, jam on the brakes, run with her to a house! But they all looked dark. Another turn, then another. And suddenly he had to put the full strength of his leg on the brake. A dead-end—the woods!

He tried to U-turn, but the car refused to gather quick speed.

He whirled to her. "Run!"

He whipped off his seatbelt but she was struggling with hers. He raced around to her side. She was still trying to unhook it as the headlights arced into the street and came blazing closer. He pulled the belt free; she stumbled out.

A house! Race up to one of the houses! But here too all of them were dark. He grabbed her hand and ran with her to the grass that fronted the woods. He started to head deep into them but suddenly she was pulling back in panic. He started pulling her again but she was trying to run another way, just along the inside of the woods. He yielded to her panic and they ran among the brush and trees at the fringe of it, until she stumbled against him, fell. They ran a little farther, then sagged behind a cluster of trees. All they could do was pull in breaths.

She'd lost a shoe and pulled off the other one. She leaned against him, gasping.

Suddenly his hand went over her mouth. He saw the approaching flicker of a flashlight, fragmented by the trees it was raking. And somewhere behind the light came the sounds of twigs snapping underfoot, and brush pushed aside. He eased her to her feet. He started to inch with her toward the street but quickly saw that a chain-link fence blocked the way. He tugged her to follow him deeper into the woods but soon she was tugging back in panic again, drawing him to her. Then she clutched at her temples and slumped to her knees.

"I—I don't—" She kept shaking her head.

He clasped her to him, his hand on the back of her head. He kept stroking her, looking around. The light was flickering closer. Then it stopped, began flying around, then the light and the sounds started moving in another direction, deep into the woods. But soon Ben saw bits of the light flying again, coming back.

His hand on her mouth, long enough to urge silence,

he lifted her again. He led her through the trees, parallel to where he thought the fence must be. Then they had to sag down again. The trees were farther apart here; he could peer through them out to the street, and didn't see a fence.

The street lay about fifteen yards from the trees.

It was tempting just to run out there.

He couldn't see the flashlight anymore, didn't hear the sounds—just the insect hums and buzzes of the woods that he hadn't noticed before. Raindrops splattered on them from the trees. They couldn't go back to the car, the guy could be waiting there. Or he could be hiding along the edge of the woods, waiting for them to run out. There were streetlights out there, but in the haze their gleam was closer to darkness than to light. It was probably only after ten at most, but from here, from this angle, he could see only one house with lights on. But there had to be others.

He straightened slowly. She looked at him, holding his hand.

A phone—he could make out what looked to be a phone at the end of the block.

He kneeled down again. "Listen," he whispered, "I'm going to try a house, and I think there's a phone farther down. You want to wait here?"

"No!" She shook her head quickly. She was shivering, hands clasped under her face.

"Nan, he could be waiting for us to come out."

She kept shaking her head.

He led her, crouched over, to a tree closest to the street.

He said, "All right. All right now. Just tell me when."

She drew in a breath, but it was more a series of

gasps. Then she lowered her head, took in another breath, and looked at the street. And then she nodded.

Holding her by the hand he ran across the grass and into the street and up the steps of the nearest house. He rang the bell, pounded on the door, then after a few moments helped her over the low railing to the adjoining open porch. He rang that bell hard, and just then the door to the first house opened just enough for someone to peer out, then that door went closed fast. He rang this bell again, then once more, then scampered with her down the steps. They ran along the sidewalk to the phone—it was outside a darkened store, near a street lamp.

He fumbled for change, though he didn't know if you needed any for 911.

"Police!" He was clutching her close as he spoke into the phone. "We need 'em fast!"

"Where," oh, so calmly, "are you?"

Oh Christ! He looked at Nancy. "Where are we?" and she hurried away, long enough to make sure, and told him what corner they were on. And now, his arm around her, they waited with their backs against the door of the store.

A patrol car pulled up in a few minutes. "Did you get a license number?"

"No." He shook his head.

"How about the make of car?"

"No."

"You see who was in it?"

"No, there was no way."

The officer strode back to his car, to the radio, and soon sirens were converging from the distance. And as other patrol cars pulled up, to speed off again, and another officer was getting information from them, a

civilian car drew to the curb and Ed Gowan stepped
out.

After a quick, surprised look at them, and a few
words with a patrolman, he walked over to them. "Jesus," to Ben after a nod at Nancy, "I was up at the
house and heard all the sirens." He was wearing bedroom slippers under slacks and an open, light windbreaker. He'd put on his gun. "Tell me what's happening."

Ben told him quickly, then something that he'd just
started thinking about: "Cassaway—she could be in
particular danger tonight. This is the first time we
know of that this guy's blown it. He didn't make it a
suicide, a hit-and-run, an accident— He's out in the
open now. I don't know who the hell's on his list next
but I'm positive Cassaway has to be one of them. And
she's got to know. And she's got to know tonight."

Gowan looked at him. "Let me decide that. One
thing, I'm not waking her up just to tell her that. I'll
take a look at the house, see if it's dark. If it is I'll
see her tomorrow."

"She ought to know tonight. This guy's blown it
and he's floating around, and for all he knows we've
got his license plate number and he's got nothing to
lose. And he is crazy."

Gowan's eyes flared. "I'm telling you I'll see."

"Well, while you're the hell seeing I'm telling this
guy!" He pointed at the officer standing by the one
patrol car still at the curb. "Or I'll go myself, I'm not
going to sleep thinking this guy could just ring her
bell and she might open the door!" Ben started to
walk to the cop, but Gowan grabbed his arm. Ben
yanked it free, whirled at him, but Gowan was mo-
tioning take it easy, take it easy.

"All right," he said. Then to Nancy: "You up to coming with us? I don't want her opening the door and seeing me and dropping dead. I don't want to live with that at church."

Ben said to her, "You up to it?"

She nodded silently and Ben joined the walk to Gowan's car. He waited until she got in the back and he slid in next to her. He put his arm through hers and held her hard as Gowan started the car. She gave several little shivers—she was wet and in stocking feet.

Ben said, "Nancy, how about you going home? We'll drop you off."

"No." She looked at him almost angrily. She didn't shiver again, seemed to be holding herself firm against it.

At Cassaway's house she quickly followed him out of the car and held onto his arm even harder. Gowan walked up the steps first. There was a faint light behind the drapes. He looked at Ben with a slight frown and shake of his head before pressing the doorbell. He waited, then took a step back and looked up at the second floor. It was dark. He rang again.

"We're gonna scare the hell out of her," he said with a scowl, then looked quickly at the door. There was the sound of the chain being released, then the doorknob turned. The door opened partway. Catherine Cassaway stood staring at them, eyes wide, mouth open.

"Miss Cassaway, Ed Gowan. Sorry to bother you. You know Nancy, Ben Newman? There's no problem, everything's okay, but I was wondering if we could come in for a minute."

She opened the door a little wider and he walked in. Ben followed Nancy. As Ben stepped in he saw with a leap of alarm Nancy's hand fly to her mouth, and Gowan standing half-turned as though frozen— and then, facing them off to the side, a thin man with black hair holding out a revolver with two hands, arms straight, rigid.

TWENTY-EIGHT

CIRCLING THEM SLOWLY, the man closed the door, then with a little flick of the gun motioned Catherine Cassaway to the sofa.

A stranger, a complete stranger!

His face, this couldn't be the face Leopold's would have grown into!

"You. You. You." He kept jabbing the gun toward the three of them. "Turn. Turn!"

Ben, watching him, was the last to turn around.

"Hands on the wall. The wall!"

Ben could feel a hand patting him for a weapon, then with a glance saw the hand patting Nancy. Then suddenly there was a cry, "You a cop? A cop?" and the hand was quickly lifting up Gowan's gun, and as Gowan turned slightly, the man, almost a blur now, began smashing at him with the gun, and Gowan was sinking to the floor, blood streaming down his face and the sides of his head. He sat slumped back against the wall, moaning, holding a limply-angled right hand and rocking over it.

"Turn around! You two, turn!" And Nancy and Ben turned, their backs to the wall, so that all four of them were within the sweep of the two guns he held now. Catherine Cassaway was slumped forward on the sofa, clutching her temples.

He looked at Ben, Nancy and Gowan closely, then only at Ben. And though it was a stranger looking at him, no one Ben recognized from that class, and though the nose was straight and narrow and the chin firm, there was something about him—in the eyes, the shape of the face, the voice—that revealed something of long ago and made it…a fixed-over face. And now despite all the changes it became Leopold's face, became set as Leopold's.

"Ben-jamin." His chest, sunken, was rising and falling. "Ben-jamin." Then the guns swung to Nancy and Gowan. "I never"—he struggled for breath— "wanted to hurt no one innocent! I never meant to, but now I can't help it, it's too late!" His guns were on Ben again, though his eyes darted to Catherine Cassaway.

"I asked you!" he demanded of her. "Tell me! Did you read those papers, those newspapers? You read about 'em?"

Hands still on her head, she nodded, then shook her head, kept shaking it.

"No? Not about what happened to your wonderful goody-goodies? Georgie-Porgy? Ell-en? Joo-ia? Alan? 'Miss *Cass*away. Miss Cass-away.' Your pets! But me—I was a slob, I was never going to amount to anything. Remember? Remember telling me?"

She kept shaking her head, eyes squeezed closed.

"'You're never going to amount to anything.' You don't remember saying that? After school, you kept me after school? And I wasn't the only one talking! 'You're never going to amount to anything!'" He leaned toward her, glaring. "Nothing!" He whirled back to Ben. "And you." He was breathing harshly through his mouth. "You. Ben-jamin." He began talking in a falsetto voice. "'*He* did it, Miss Cassaway. Aren't I a good boy for reporting him, Miss Cassaway?' 'Give out the books, Ben-jamin. You're a good boy, Ben-jamin.'"

"Leo-Leopold." It came from Miss Cassaway, her eyes still closed, her hands still against her head. And it came as more of a sound than a name.

He whirled on her. "Don't call me that! He's dead! He's gone! Don't call me that, you hear? Hear?" He kept glaring at her, then at the others, then back at her. Something seemed to go out of his body now; it looked almost limp. "I—I worked—I worked so hard. You don't know how hard." Suddenly his eyes were full of tears. He wiped them with his wrist, then ran his wrist across his nose, and for the first time Ben saw a trace of the cherry red of his gums. "I tried so hard," he said, gasping slightly. "My whole life—it could have been so different. You even—"

He wiped across his eyes again, hard. Rage came back to his voice, his whole body.

"You even— You even— 'He could've tied her up, he could have touched that little girl, he could have done awful things to her, I saw him play with her, he's weird.' You told 'em, I heard someone say it. And I never did it, I never touched her, I never hurt no one. I—I once tried to talk to her in the yard because— because she looked scared. But you told 'em. And they— 'Tell us, why'd you take her in the woods? You went inside her panties? You touch her with your thing? Why'd you take her there? Tell us and nothin's gonna happen to you.' I couldn't even live here any- more. I had to go to— I had to go to home after home."

Ben could feel Nancy's arm go under his, then

squeeze it hard. Leopold immediately swung his guns at her.

"Put that arm down! Put it down!"

But she held his arm to her even tighter. She was crying quietly now.

"Down! Put it down!"

Her arm came down slowly. Then she began shaking her head, eyes closed, tears trickling down.

"I know you didn't," she said. "I know."

The words seemed to echo in the sudden silence.

"I know," she said again, her voice choked.

She opened her eyes. Gasping, she looked at Gowan. He was still rocking over his busted hand, the blood in thick rivulets from his head, his smashed-open nose. His eyes turned to her through the blood.

"We"—she was directing it at Gowan, almost in a monotone now—"we always used to go in there. A certain part of it. And one day she showed up and—" Her eyes turned slowly to Ben. "We wanted to scare her so she'd never come back. Didn't see us. Tied her hands. Told her she was"—she was crying now—"she was never going to see her—her mommy again, that we had her on the moon, did she know where the moon was, that she was a million miles away. And we put mud on her, put it in her hair, her face, and then let her run— It was so cruel"—she was sobbing now—"it was so cruel. I can't believe how cruel—" Her hand came up to her forehead, and after a few moments, when she lowered her hand, her voice became that monotone again, still directed at Ben: "When I heard Miss Cassaway told you she thought it was—him—I called Ed, I said if that's what they had on—this person, if that was going to be a part of it, then we'd, I wasn't going to let it— And maybe, I don't know, maybe that's why he called you, to see, to watch. It's been so much on my mind, it's been eating at me. Then I made up my mind I was going to tell you. Tonight. Of all nights,'' she said, shaking her head dazedly, ''tonight.''

Ben, starting to bend toward her, was somehow remembering in the midst of all this how she'd kept pulling him away from running deeper into the woods, maybe away from that place.

''You!'' Leopold screamed, and Ben felt a gun against his forehead. It remained pressed against him as he straightened slowly, his insides contracted. Leopold drew it back a little, then swung slightly to Miss Cassaway.

''You! Blamed me! Everything me!''

Hands clasped over her ears, she was staring at him wildly.

''Everything me! You witch! You bitch! Hurt me— a kid, just a *kid,* a boy, you bitch, you—''

All at once she let out a shriek and was on her feet, rigid, screaming at him, jabbing a finger at him. He seemed paralyzed for a moment, the guns wavering. And in that instant Ben leaped and grabbed both his wrists and rushed him back against the wall, one of the guns dropping at the impact. Ben tried to force the other hand against the window, at the same time punching him with his other fist, butting him. Ben had him against the window now, kept hitting that gun hand against the glass, barely with any force at first, then harder, and the glass broke and Ben started to push his hand through it, but the gun fell. Ben smashed him on the face and he staggered back, and then when he came forward, one fist bloody, Ben had the eerie flash of being back in that schoolyard with him, because Leopold's swings were like slaps now. Ben hit him on the mouth and he dropped, and though he staggered up after several moments it was just to teeter in a daze. Ben, feeling he could just push him over, bent quickly to pick up one of the guns to keep it on him while they called the police.

But in that instant there was an intermingled scream and the blast of a gun. A gush of blood spread on Leopold's chest, and now Catherine Cassaway was standing close to him, still screaming and firing, a second bullet hitting him as he was collapsing, two others spraying the wall.

Ben leaped at her, seized her wrists, his fingers hard around them. And despite all they'd gone through, and with Pat dead, and George and Ellen and Julia and who-knew-who else, his first thought was: *You've murdered him, you bitch, you've murdered him!*

TWENTY-NINE

HIS HANDS SLIPPING from Miss Cassaway's he looked over at Nancy, who was standing slumped against the wall. He went over to her but she stood staring down, her body rigid, her hands clenched at her waist. He put his arm around her but she didn't look up. She didn't seem to know he was there.

He could hear voices outside, and then the sound of whimpering inside. Miss Cassaway was on the sofa, bent toward her knees, the whimpering turning into gasps. And Gowan, who was huddled on his knees, was straightening up now, was walking over to her, bent over, his good hand cradling the bad.

He sat down heavily, next to her; was leaning toward her and saying something softly.

The only thing Ben heard was: "...took courage."

Then he saw her trembling hand come over and squeeze his.

Ben led Nancy out, into the wide, bright beams of police cars, and with crowds far back on either side. No, to a cop, he wasn't hurt. No, said Nancy, no.

Two or three police vans came, one for the sheeted mound that was Leopold's body, another for Gowan and Cassaway to step into, she with help on both sides. Nancy and Ben were sped off in a patrol car for questioning by detectives.

She sat silently, fingers intertwined on her lap, not looking at him, even when he put his arm around her. And even when he said, "Let it go. It was long ago, let it go."

PART OF Leopold's story was to come from a scattering of people who'd known him. After leaving Philadelphia, he'd first surfaced in Indianapolis, at the age of thirteen, where he was picked up for breaking into abandoned houses. He was sent to a juvenile facility, then lived in a group home, where he got into a program that sent him to a vocational school. He then held a few jobs as a TV repairman, the final one at a shop owned by an elderly childless couple named Fred and Delores Harris, who took him into their home, did everything but formally adopt him. Several years later they were killed in a boating accident, which left him devastated. He tried at one point to run the shop but, according to witnesses, seemed barely able to function, and disappeared after about a month.

No one knew where he went after that, except that a couple of years later he showed up in St. Louis, where he officially changed his name and underwent extensive plastic surgery—the final denial of being Leopold anymore. No one knew exactly when he returned to Philadelphia, just that he'd rented his present apartment about four months ago.

As far as anyone knew, he'd never married, was always known as "quiet"—in fact, seemed especially liked by children and had no adult criminal record.

The remaining bits and pieces of his story came from a composition book found in his apartment. It was, as most of the newspapers commented, one of those black-and-white marbleized books every child has used. And everything was hand-printed carefully, clearly, without a single mistake, as though he'd squeezed agonizingly hard on the ballpoint pen to get it just right.

There were details—just a few words, but details—of the five murders, including Alan Green's, whose body was somewhere in the New Jersey pinelands but hadn't as yet been found. Referring to Pat, he wrote that her death was "an accident I couldn't help," and concluded it with, in capital letters: *I AM NOT DUMB*.

There were also fragments of "thoughts"—how he'd always brooded about Cassaway and "the kids she liked," blaming them for his suffering, his problems, but never more than after the deaths of the Harrises. In Philadelphia, apparently, he'd spent quite a bit of time wandering around Barwyn, undoubtedly drawn to it as to an ache. And it was there, his notes said, that seeing the picture of George Havers set off the killings.

And there was a quiet kind of ranting, too, about how he was as smart as any of those kids; but nothing about why he was writing this down, though police and a couple of psychiatrists who were quoted in the newspapers felt that he'd originally intended showing the composition book to Miss Cassaway—so neat, finally something perfect—before he killed her.

But the line from the book that was headlined in most news stories was: *MY NAME IS CHARLES HARRIS. I WANT IT ON MY GRAVE.*

BEN PICKED UP the phone quickly, hoping it was Nancy. But it was Harry, from his office. "I was wondering," Harry said, "did you reach her?"

"Not yet." He hadn't seen Nancy since they'd left

the detectives, a couple of days ago. One of her employees said she'd gone away for a few days.

Harry was silent for a moment. Then, "Ben, what more can I say about you? You're a good guy. Quite a guy."

"That's saying enough." At times, growing up, he'd have died to hear it.

"I was such a pain in the ass. And here you were working for me. And I didn't believe anything you said. Didn't even hear it, I mean. Went in one ear and out the other."

"You had enough to think about."

"But there's one thing I'm still angry about. You didn't tell me this guy was after you. Why didn't you ever tell me?"

"You had enough on your mind." *And,* Ben thought, *you probably wouldn't have really heard that, either.*

"It scares me just thinking about it. You should have, Ben. Christ, I'm your brother, we're brothers."

"We are that, Harry. And I love you." It came out so easily, though it had been years since either of them said it.

"You know I love you, too. Look, I'll be calling you this evening."

"Sure." But Ben almost smiled. If it was still the old Harry, he might call, but he probably wouldn't. But that was okay. It made things normal again. "I'll talk to you, Harry," he said.

He stood up from the phone and sat at his desk, where the morning paper was strewn across it. Still front page.

He'd given the cops the exact sequence leading to Leopold's death, letting them decide whether Miss

Cassa-way had deliberately shot bullet after bullet or had fired in hysteria. But Nancy, he'd seen in this morning's *Dispatch*, had come right out and said she didn't have to do it. Nancy had also admitted the incident with Betsie, though the paper described it only as a "prank she'd done with another pupil that the dead man thought people blamed him for."

Gowan, on the other hand, said that Miss Cassaway acted out of "great courage and instinct."

Neither he nor Miss Cassaway said anything about the "prank."

And in today's paper, Ben saw, Danny Haupt was quoted as saying that she was to receive a special award at the bicentennial.

He couldn't remember ever feeling so goddamn sad.

About Pat and George and Ellen and Alan and Julia. And Nancy, carrying Betsie with her all these years. And even about Catherine Cassaway, though he detested her, who would always think she'd done the best for her kids, and perhaps had for most.

Not Gowan at all, he loathed the guy, and didn't mind seeing those innuendoes in the paper—cop loses gun, and maybe his rung on the ladder. Then there was Leopold—Leopold. Not that black-haired guy with the altered face—Leopold had been right, that wasn't really Leopold. But that awkward kid with the snotty nose, in foster home after foster home, and out there in that schoolyard, slapping at him like a girl.

A few words? Could he have saved Leopold with just a few words, or by walking home with him from school? Ben went over and sat on the arm of a lounge chair near the window.

Had he been any different from Shumlin, afraid to risk? Or all that much bolder than Danny, fixed in his

grandfather's store? Or Nevon, even Nevon, afraid
enough to be willing to shit purple?

Joannie's "hippie" uncle. Yeah.

NANCY PHONED HIM a couple of hours later.

"Nan, where are you?"

"Still away," she said. "I just grabbed up some
things and ran. Actually, I'm at the Jersey shore, it
doesn't matter where. I've rented a little cottage on
the beach and though it's lonely, I have to be alone
for a while. I've got to think myself out a little. Big
secret, I don't think all that much of myself. Never
have."

"You must," he said, "be jesting."

"And you," she said, "are being very nice."

"Well, you've just got to do a lot of rethinking
then."

"I'll try."

"Say 'I will.'"

"I will." He could detect a smile as she said it.

He said, "Tell me, did anyone give you a rough
time over what you said about Cassaway?"

"Oh, screw 'em all. They think she's a great hero.
I'm finally getting out of Barwyn anyway. Once and
for all. That much I've decided. God, it's time."

"You sound mighty happy saying that."

"Oh, I am. Well," she said then, "I just wanted
you to hear from me. I'm sorry I just disappeared. And
I'll call you again soon, either from here or home."

"Okay." But he had to smile. That sounded like
Harry. But she wasn't Harry.

HE LET THE answering machine take the rest of the
calls. One was from Carter Svenson, who said,

"What's this I've been reading out of your city? And about you? Murders that go back to *grammar* school? Call me, please. I've even got the title—it's a natural—'Whose Name On My Grave?'"

He hoped Carter would understand his stepping aside on this one. This was going to be his second book.

But a call he did take came through about six that evening. He picked up the phone, knowing it was McGlynn, at the word "Kid."

Ben said, "Bill. Hi."

"Hey, how you doing there, kid? I'm just calling to see how you are."

"I'm doing real well."

"Good. Good. Look, I just want to say I'm glad I was able to be of some help." And as Ben started to look up at the ceiling, "The problem was, you know, it wasn't my case. And some guys get mighty touchy."

"I understand."

"You know something?" McGlynn sounded hesitant. "I was just saying to the wife. I really was. I was saying I wish I was you."

"You wish you were me? Really?"

"Sure, really. You can really write, kid. And on top of it all, on top of that, you got a cop's head."

TO
PERISH
IN
PENZANCE

A DOROTHY MARTIN MYSTERY
JEANNE M. DAMS

While Dorothy Martin loves nearly everything about England, the lure
of the sunshine of Cornwall's picturesque coast...and an unsolved
mystery, prove too tempting to resist.

Thirty years earlier, the murder of a beautiful woman became her husband's
first homicide investigation. The case was never solved. Upon their arrival,
Dorothy and Alan meet a young woman who turns out to be the daughter
of that long-ago victim. Tragically, Lexa shares the same fate as her
mother when she, too, is found dead on the rocky shores of Penzance.

In a town teeming with legends and lore, Dorothy vows to avenge two
innocent deaths, and bring a clever killer to justice.

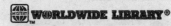

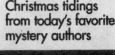